Halloween Screams

By

The Globe Writers.

About the Authors.

The Globe Writers are a collection of published and unpublished authors that meet on Tuesday nights at the Globe coffee shop in Cleethorpes. There are a wide range of talents, from poets to novelists, with focuses on different genres. They have banded together again for this horror anthology. Enjoy!

Also, by the same authors:

Christmas Gifts.

Tales from Lockdown.

She Wolf.

By Lord Stabdagger.

The forest was still in the early hours of a cold autumn morning. The silence was broken only by the breeze through the trees and the restless trickling of a stream running through the middle of a clearing. A ghostly mist slowly danced over the dew sodden ground faintly illuminated by the failing glow of the moon overhead, obscured by a veil of thickening clouds. Nothing moved apart from the crystal-clear water. No creature made a sound, and yet among the dark shadows a pair of watchful eyes peered over the clearing and observed the scene with extreme caution, studying every detail as though hunting for any signs of life. The slightest movement or sound, the smallest disturbance would mean potential danger. She was weak, hurt and vulnerable.

A gap in the clouds passed over the moon and temporally brightened the scene. A faint rustle from beneath fallen leaves nearby caused her body to tense, probably just a rodent, but she couldn't afford to be careless. With great courage she dared to step her paw slowly and as silently as she was able from behind the overgrowth, placing it on the cold ground with the gentlest touch, then froze again to re assess the danger. With the trickling water beckoning her, she cautiously moved out of her hiding place, and crept toward the stream, each step as delicate and as deliberate as the first. Her grey and white fur was wet with dew and blood. She limped from a savage injury to her hind leg with her tail between them. Her body battered yet her spirit defiant.

A strong gust of wind hit the trees and made them hiss. Somewhere a branch cracked, and she stopped motionless again, crouched lower, ready to run with the last of her effort. Another fight now would surely be her last. Her tattered ears erect and her nose twitching, she waited until confident she was still alone, then crept closer to the stream until she stood at its edge.

The smell of the fresh clean water filled her nose with pure delight. Her mouth pined for its sweet taste as she heartily lapped it up, yet she coughed and spluttered. Each time she tried to swallow her throat burned. Such was the ferocity of the previous night with several sets of jaws trying to leave their mark, yet her need compelled her to carry on. With every drop she managed to down, the near freezing temperature seemed to numb the agony. It was little relief.

After drinking as much as she was able, she stood on trembling limbs and again observed the surrounding area. The night was beginning to brighten. The wind had picked up a touch passing thousands of smells and odours by her snout, the many scents of the forest and the freshness of the air. The hiss of the trees and trickling water was becoming faint as her ears were succumbing to an increasing tinnitus. Only the sound of her heart remained audible as a rapid relentless beat.

She steadily walked into the water until she found a shallow place somewhere in the middle. It was so cold it stung on the pads of her paws, yet the increasing sensation of tension throughout her body and her near total exhaustion made her care little for any more pain.

Enough was enough. Panting deeply, she looked at her wavering reflection as the moon found another gap to shine through. Her snout was covered in cuts and gashes that wept with blood. Her right eye was swollen, her left ear was torn; the clear water was obscured with trickles of blood as the many wounds all over her body bled.

Her limbs grew weak. She slowly lowered until she was lying in the water. One final look around, and she curled herself up, laying her head on her paws to keep her snout out of the water, then gradually, her eyes closed as a strong numbing sensation spread through her whole body, eliminating the pain and the biting cold of the stream.

The night passed. The wind eased. The mist continued to creep steadily over the ground. The birds had long since begun to sing yet none flew over the clearing where the stream trickled over rocks and stones. Gradually, from out of the surrounding forest, various animals began to dare their way toward the stream as they do every morning. Today, their instincts told them to stay away. Something wasn't right. Among the animals was a stag, Leader of a group of deer. It sensed something, potential danger, yet his group needed refreshment. He dared to step towards the stream until he stood by the edge. Everything seemed normal, except for what looked like a new rock in the middle of the water. All around the scene was clumps of white and grey fur flickering in the breeze. There was an unfamiliar smell that his instincts told him was something to be cautious of.

His thirst was great. He looked back the way he came, twitching his ears and licking his lips; then dipped his mouth to drink. As he did other members of his group hurriedly yet quietly came up to join in. as more came, he walked further into it, getting closer to the new rock. The strange smell was coming from it, and it was covered in more of the wispy fur being blown away by the breeze. He sniffed around it then dared to gently nudge it. As he did it moved. Instantly the group of deer's ran back to the forest. The stag stopped just before disappearing and looked back. The rock was a young human woman looking back at him with wild fearful eyes through strands of long wet hair.

She watched the stag leap into the overgrowth and vanish. Shivering, naked and weary, she looked around her. Amongst the residual physical pain from her catalogue of injuries, she felt a sense of great relief. She was alive and alone. Her wounds had closed but no doubt she would have left a strong trail for the others to follow by the scent of her blood. It won't take them long to find her. Exhausted or not she had to keep moving, had to give herself the chance to heal and gather her strength to face them again. One more fight should do it. Another victory and they will be the ones running.

She looked at her reflection. Her pretty face will have scars, as will her throat, chest and the rest of her body, a small price to pay for what she's fighting for. Her eyes were still the eyes of the wolf. She cupped her hands and splashed her face several times until her reflection showed them to be human again.

Four weeks until the next full moon. Four weeks to avoid the others and be weary of the humans. She looked hard at her wavering face in the water. She had nothing to lose now, yet everything to gain.

Falling for a Witch Hunter.

By

Gemma Owen Kendall.

Golden brown are the colours I see upon the trees from my walk home tonight, the rustling sound of dead leaves as I stroll along the path, crunch, crunch. It is the middle of October already, the year is going by so quickly. Everyone at college is telling me that it will soon be Christmas but I'm not ready to think about the season of goodwill. My main focus is to think about Halloween, it is the time of year for witches to appear, the jack-a-lanterns to be lit and for the monsters to roam the streets. I'm not scared at all, this time of year always intrigues me. For you see I am secretly a witch myself, I learnt to be one from my grandmother. I don't have a cauldron or a black cat like you see in Sabrina, The Teenage Witch. I'm more into healing spells and bringing good to the town I live in. My powers are just stronger throughout October. I recently found out that I'm being hunted by a witch hunter, I saw him follow me home the other night. Problem is I know him very well, this guy was my crush in secondary school. Tall, dark haired and very handsome with a cheeky grin, his name is Adam and I can always sense him nearby, this is one of my gifts for being a witch. I even recognise his footsteps on my walk this evening as I pass by a local coffee shop that is open late, the linger of pumpkin spiced lattes aroma through the air. I gaze in quickly through the steamed up window and see a young couple sat together, John and Jenny. They were mates of mine in school, now and again I will receive the odd text from Jenny mentioning about meeting up soon for a catch up but I know most of her time is spent with John. They only started dating when we finished school, John was my first and only boyfriend in school but we broke up only after six weeks of being together. Nothing too serious happened in that time luckily but he was my first kiss. When I found out about him and Jenny, I couldn't have been more happy for them, I was too fixated on pining for Adam all the time. I paused by the window to try get their attention but they were to engrossed with each other to notice me.

A gloved hand then covers my mouth and I feel the blade of a sharp object, cold, touching the base of my throat. Whoever this is drags me to the nearest alleyway and pushes me up against the rough bricked wall slightly banging the back of my head. From the silhouette in the dusk light I can see this figure is male, he pulls down his hood from his sweater to reveal who he is. The look of anger upon his face scares me, vengeful red glaring eyes piece through me, I feel the tears start to fall from my eyes.

"What are you crying for witch." He hisses at me, feeling the spit from his words landing on my face. I squint my eyes shut in the hopes whatever this guy wants from me, he will just get it over with pretty quickly. "Look at me, witch."

"Let her go." Another male voice yells in the distance, I know that voice all too well but surely it can't be him, the witch hunter. I hear a quick scuffle and then I'm released from the clutches of this evil person, I refuse to open my eyes still so I huddle into a ball. I hear a loud roar and then a warm sticky substance lands on me. "It's ok now, you can open your eyes." I do as I am commanded, the state was unbearable to look at, Adam was standing over me with a blooded axe with his other hand offering to help me stand. I reciprocate with my hand and let him help me onto my feet, he drops his axe, the sound of metal hitting the concrete floor goes through me. Flinching, he gently pulls me into his arms, I try to resist his pull not knowing whether or not he is going to kill me. He senses my restrain from his embrace.

"I'm not going to hurt you." He soothes at me

"How do I know you won't when you are a witch hunter." I hiss back at him

"I've had many chances to kill you if I wanted to."

"Then why haven't you?"

"Cos I love you, Lucy."

The sound of him saying those words and my name in one sentence struck my heart, I have always loved him and it was wonderful to know he felt the same way towards me. This was so against who we were, the witch falling for the witch hunter. The witch hunters are destined to kill us witches, there was no way we would be accepted of being together by society but right now I didn't care, I just wanted to be with Adam and only him. My heart belongs to him. I let him pull me back into his arms, placing my hand onto his right cheek. I could just see the outline of his facial features down the dark alley way, still as handsome as he ever was back in school.

"I love you too." I whispered back to him. He placed his lips gently onto mine, my stomach somersaulting three times, not wanting this kiss to ever end. The slow movements from our lips turned into a passionate kiss, feeling so right. Who cares if we were sworn enemies, Adam saved my life and I was completely head over heels in love with him.

"Thank you for saving my life."

"You're welcome, but we must keep this a secret for now."

"I promise, I will do everything I can to protect us."

"And I will always protect you."

A Date With Death.

By

Pauline Seawards.

Halloween is all about portals. The lifting of the veil between life and death. Is it a one way passage. We, the living, remember the visitations of ghosts but do they remember visiting us?

Do ghosts even exist?

I'd say they are rare and elusive, improbable even, but can't be ruled out altogether.

Grimsby: October 31st. Halloween eve.

The clocks went back a week ago and its dark when I leave work. An hour ago I sneaked away from my desk to watch the sunset. The Victoria Flour Mills glowed like the element in a toaster.

'Why are you standing in the corridor?' a colleague asked. I told them I was looking at the view, unable to think of a better story, and I felt like a wimp. There isn't time for window gazing in that job.

Driving home the streets are teeming with groups of people. Why do they all wear black? Makes it so hard to see them. I drive very slowly, there are 'sleeping policemen' all along Park Street anyway, but no speed feels safe as people walk in the road, without care for their own safety.

Occasionally a face looks into my headlights and I see a flash of luminous bone, trickles of blood around a jaw-line.

I don't like it.

For one thing I could run someone over. For another, some of these people could be dead already. If I was dead I would definitely choose this night to pay a visit to earth. Like a celebrity wearing a hoodie I'd be hidden in plain sight, among all the fake ghouls and zombies.

I'm driving towards Five Ways when I see him and there is a rush of familiarity. A lad with a pumpkin head mask riding a bike. What the f***! Priceless, stupid. I'm doing an emergency stop and trying to swerve at the same time.

My neck jerks backwards as the car stops and a snapping sound vibrates through my skull. That isn't the last thing I hear. There are some thrilled screams as if this event has been staged for the amusement of the crowd. Then real screams, and cries of 'so much blood'. I can feel the blood, wet and sticky on my face, warm. I try to speak but my jaw is broken, and anyway I'm nearly dead now, my life ebbing away to the sound of sirens.

Every year it's the same outcome. I always think that if I drive slowly enough I'll avoid the crash. But maybe that is the wrong tactic. If I drove more quickly I might miss the pumpkin headed kid altogether. But on the other hand I might actually run him over. I wouldn't want to have that on my conscience as I slumber though eternity.

Moonlighting.

By

Tracey Gavan Johnson.

She's going to love you" she said reassuringly, smiling at him. They were driving through the thick forest and were almost at her Gran's cottage "I only mentioned it because people sometimes find her a little..."

"Eccentric?" Eric supplied helpfully.

"Hmm. I prefer unusual." She replied. "I love her for it though. I can't imagine being brought up by anyone who wasn't interesting the way she is. She is... just beautiful." She paused, smiling to herself. "Everything about her, inside and out. Like a summer day." Keeping her eye on the road, she glanced across at her companion. She stroked his knee. "It's hard to explain, but you'll get it when you meet her". She always found it difficult to find the right way, the right words to describe her Gran, the woman who raised her alone in a cottage in the middle of nowhere. She knew that her childhood had been unusual and still often felt this need to explain it to new people.

The little red Beetle continued to wind its way down the curvy path towards the cottage in the clearing where the young woman had been raised. They had lived, the two of them, secluded in the little wooden cabin that had been built many years before her birth, in a clearing hewn out of the forest itself. The cottage was surrounded on all sides by a garden teeming with plants. Some that you ate, and some that cured your ailments. People came to see her Gran, asked her advice, often leaving with a mixture to cure a pain, or a handful of herbs to soothe a worry away. As she spoke of it to friends or colleagues, she heard how unconventional her childhood sounded, how curious to the ears of others. But to the young woman, it was the only way to be raised that she knew. As a child, home-schooled by her Gran, she had few friends with which to compare her upbringing. It was only when she left home to study in the city that she had fully realised how isolated they had been. But she felt no loss at the fact. Her childhood had been the happiest; idyllic, secure. And anything she had missed in the way of companionship, was made up for with love, attention and in a myriad of other ways.

She knew this road through the heart of the forest like the back of her hand, by daylight or moonlight. It was six years since she had called the tiny cottage home and moved to the city, but she still made the trip every month to visit the woman who raised her, her beloved Gran. It was usually evening by the time she left and set off on her journey back to the city and although any street lights were far away, the forest road winding through the tall pines was enough of a familiar friend, keeping her company, guiding her on her solitary journey.

But today, this particular journey was different. They were driving in bright sunshine and she was not alone. Her passenger was Eric, the beautiful young man sitting beside her. "She raised you Rachel" he was saying now, "and you are beautiful inside and out. How could she herself be any other?" He was coiling her auburn curls around his fingers absentmindedly and smiling at her softly as he spoke and she drove.

She loved the way He said her name. He was the only person she knew who called her by it. Her Gran had always called her Red (on account of her hair she supposed) and it was how she introduced herself to everyone that she met. It was how she thought of herself and yet when He had asked, she had introduced herself as Rachel, that long ago given name that she had almost forgotten. She still wasn't sure why now, but she had said "Rachel" automatically, when he had asked her.

She had spoken of Him to her Gran of course. How beautiful and kind he was. How he might be "the One". And the strange way they had met. That unexpected and extraordinary encounter on this very road as she had been leaving Gran's and journeying back to the city after one of her monthly visits, almost a year ago now. Although it had been much after nightfall, her way had been lit by a glorious October full moon shining in a cloudless sky high above the tall, dense pines of the forest. She had been chugging along on autopilot as people tend to do on familiar journeys, humming along to the car radio. Yawning occasionally. Her

17

headlights had been illuminating the road when the moonlight was suddenly hidden by trees, and literally out of nowhere had appeared in the headlights a great furry creature, running straight across in the direct path of the car, a speeding flurry of shining dampness in the drizzle and the car headlights. Screeching the car to a holt, she sat breathless, heart-pounding, afraid to move, afraid to get out of the car and check, certain as she was that the poor creature, a dog she was sure of it, was under the wheels. The still engine hummed and Stevie Nicks crooned quietly in the background as she stared out though the windscreen in shock and then astonishment, as a beautiful young man rose from the ground in front of the bonnet.

He looked back at her and put his hands up in a gesture to indicate that he was alright and casually began to brush himself down. For a moment she sat, frozen, her hands still gripping the steering wheel and stared out as he dusted himself down and checked himself over. Still she just stared. His hair was dark brown, slightly curly and untidy, probably in need of a cut she thought inconsequentially. She suddenly interrupted her own intrusive train of thought with an image of herself running her hands through the straggly curls at the nape.

She shook herself into action. Filled with remorse and completely forgetting that she was in the middle of nowhere, now with a stranger for company, she fumbled with her seatbelt and hurried out of the car to his side.

"Oh my god, are you OK? I am so sorry. You just came out of nowhere..." She babbled on, "and where's the dog?" He'd come home in his own good time he had assured her, no longer brushing himself down, but holding her gaze with piecing green eyes. He told her there was no harm done, that he was fine. He seemed friendly, affable. Impulsively, she offered him a lift to his home. A small cabin, it turned out, on the edge of the forest on the road back to the city. She was in awe to later find out that he built it himself from scratch.

Imprudent though it had been, to offer a lift to a stranger in the dead of night, she had felt obliged to, having almost run him over. But she had not accepted his offer of a cup of coffee in his cabin before she continued her journey. Although foolhardy as that would have been, she had almost said yes, so charmed was she by this young man. But in a gush of further apologies, they had somehow exchanged numbers. Oh my days! Red had thought to herself as she drove away. So fascinated was she with the young man, she was still thinking of those green eyes and that intense gaze. "I have an actual crush!"

She had never been back to his little cabin since that night. He had never again invited her. Though they had seen each other almost every day since, they preferred to spend their time in the city. And as they spent more and more time together she realised that he was indeed very special to her. The only down side was that he never saw his dog again.

19

"So, here we are" she said now as they pulled up outside her grandmother's house. Her Gran was standing at the gate to greet them.

"So you are the famous Eric I have been hearing so much about" her Gran said as they sat on plump sofas in the main room of the cottage. Having said their hellos and introductions, tea was now poured and scones offered. "You are indeed as handsome as Red said you were."

"Gran. Don't tease" warned Red with a smile.

"Have we met before? You know I have a feeling that we have" her Gran continued pouring tea, unchastised.

"No, I'm sure I would remember" he said and smiled his charming smile.

"Then maybe I've met your family? Red tells me you live in the forest".

"Gran, Eric doesn't see his family. I told you that too". Red, not wishing him to have to answer her Gran's probing questions now shot her grandmother a cautionary look. She recognised that beady look in her Gran's eye. She was like a dog with a bone when she thought she was on to something and she did not want Eric subjected to an interrogation on his first visit. The truth was that Eric was estranged from his family. He had not said why and Red had not asked. She supposed it must cause him pain and so she had not probed him further.

Her Gran changed subjects. "Red tells me you both have a lot in common Eric. And you're vegetarian too, like Red. Now that is an interesting choice."

"It's not so unusual these days. I've told you Gran. Stop pretending to be old fashioned." said Red "Enough teasing now. Eric doesn't know you well enough yet!"

"Well we shall have to put that right shan't we?" her Gran replied smiling across at her grand -daughter. "Red, why don't you pop out and see whether the chucks have laid anything for our tea my love. I'll keep Eric occupied." She winked at him mischievously.

When Red was gone, she turned to Eric. She looked him in the eye and smiled her sweet smile. "Vegetarian? Impressive. That's very committed." She paused and nibbled around the edge of her scone. "Was that a difficult choice Eric?"

"Mostly not" He looked her in the eye and smiled back at the shrewd old woman sitting opposite him.

She paused, "And your family? How did they take it?"

He was about to take a mouthful of scone. "As Rachel... Red", he corrected himself, "mentioned, I don't have anything, to do with my family. Anything at all" he reiterated. They both chewed and drank for a silent moment.

"And do you take medication for your little condition Eric?" She looked him frankly in the eye. "For your sake and my grand-daughter's I hope that you do."

Eric stared back for a moment. He swallowed the mouthful of scone, which had suddenly and inexplicably changed into a mouthful of sand, so dry that he had to swill it down with a gulp of the tea. In just that moment he was sure. She knew. His eyes were glinting. Several emotions flitted across his retina before he settled on one. He took a deep breath. There was no question about it. 'Gran' was it seemed, who he had suspected she might be. He stared across at this new and powerful adversary.

He cleared his throat. "Yes. Of course. Every month at the full moon. Without fail. It is what I have … chosen."

"Well that's a relief to hear Eric. Though I have heard it does not work for everyone" she said. She raised her teacup to her lips and waited.

"It works for me." he replied. "Without fail. I assure you". "That is good news I'm sure" she paused to wander over to the window to watch her grand -daughter in the garden. "Often the old remedies are the most effective" she mused. "As Red may have told you, I have a way with herbs myself. I have many cures, for numerous ailments. And I often find that there's more than one way to skin a cat. Or a wolf for that matter". Pausing, she sipped her tea and turned to him. "And did you know who she was? Red? At first?"

"No" he replied honestly. "Not at first. Not for sure until now".

"And yet here she is. Safe and sound. That reassures me a great deal Eric." She smiled suddenly. Though it didn't quite reach her eyes. "So, I do believe that as long as you take your medicine young man, you and I shall get along fine". She smiled and sipped again. "Now, I hope you'll stay for dinner?"

AAA Exorcisms and House Blessings.

By Ants Ambridge.

The street was silent. Not a car nor person made their way down the suburban lane containing 16 Lewisham Drive. A heavy fog had descended on the town, bathing it in a murk, despite it being early morning. The fog parted to allow Father McKinley to stride with purpose down the drive of the semi-detached property and rap curtly on the door.

Mrs Crowley opened the door to greet him, dark rings under her eyes through a lack of sleep. Her hair dishevelled, adding to her frazzled appearance. Relief washed over her face as she spotted Father McKinley's dog collar.

- Father! I'm so glad you came!
- Hello my child. My tea has four sugars.
- Can we not get started?
- Bless ye, I can't be reading my blessings with a cracked and dry throat, can I now? One messed up word and it could turn a mere presence into a category 4 poltergeist. And you're not wanting that now, are yis?
- No, no, I suppose not. Please come in.

McKinley clomped into the foyer and perused his surroundings with an air of expertise. Mrs Crowley shuffled through to her kitchen and flicked on the kettle. McKinley tapped on the wall and inhaled through his teeth. Mrs Crowley stepped from the kitchen, puzzled by his reaction.

- Have ye had another priest visit before me?
- Yes, Father, the vicar from the local parish said a blessing last week.
- Bloody proddy dogs. He's made a right balls-up of it. There's ectoplasm on the stairs.
- That has been coming through the walls since before he came. Can you stop it? It's terrifying.
- See, there's the thing. I can, but it will take a while. I'll need a few visits. Best I can manage is a temporary solution.
- And what's that?
- I've got a bucket in my van. Where is Mr Crowley?
- He took our son to stay with his mother until we've eliminated the problems. I needed to stay…

McKinley raised a hand to silence her. A faint buzzing increased in volume, and a black mass grew in the window. Flies gathered, covering the windowpanes, eliminating the little light that came in. The front door, only recently closed, flew open and a guttural voice echoed through the hallway.

- GET OUT!!

Mrs Crowley yelped in fright. McKinley chuckled in response.

- He's a feisty little bollocks and no mistake! Although not entirely original! They probably only get poorly paced horror films from the 80s in the foul depths of hell. Figures!

McKinley opened his worn bible and read a passage in a booming voice, almost losing his Irish accent completely as he did so. The flies coating the window dissipated, and Mrs Crowley's breathing became less shallow. After a brief genuflection, McKinley clapped his hands together, wiping off imaginary dust.

- Job done! Is that tea ready yet, missus?
- That's one part of the problem father, did my husband not explain on the phone?
- Ye'll haff to forgive me, I'm a bit of a forgetful knacka. So many jobs, you understand?
- Well, there is the front bedroom. It's best I show you...
- Lead the way. After the cuppa.

Mrs Crowley tutted and obliged. She handed McKinley a steaming mug and motioned for him to follow her upstairs. McKinley took a noisy slurp of tea and winked.

- Ah, that's grand. God's nectar.

They made the short walk across the landing, and with a trembling hand, reached for the door handle on the front bedroom. She pushed it open and stepped back. The half-grin fell from McKinley's face. A single bed hovered in the centre of the room, toys spinning around. An action figure pranced in a circle, a tinny, shrieking laugh emanating from its tiny mouth. As it danced, its foot hit a spinning Lego brick, and the laugh became a howl, shocking both with the ferocity of the volume. A stuffed clown paused in front of their widened eyes, grabbing a headless Barbie and prying the legs apart and thrusting in a vulgar parody of the act of love. McKinley, now shaking as much as Mrs Crowley pulled the door closed with a slam. He smoothed his shirt down with his hand. Composed, he turned back to Mrs Crowley with a smile.

- Dat's a hell of a draught coming through in there! I guess yis need to call the double-glazing people!
- What are you talking about? That's clearly a poltergeist!
- That's a common misconception. I see this kind of thing all the time! Draughts can be a powerful force!
- The toys were dancing!
- Trick o' the eyes. That's all there is! You call the window fellas, and if they don't sort it, I'll come back and take another look. But mark my words, that's the problem right there!

Mrs Crowley wanted to argue. Her head even wobbled a little, but she had more pressing matters on her mind. She pushed for the main reason she had called the priest here.

27

- Father, what we most need your help with... is... is... my daughter. We fear she is possessed. Of the devil.

Father McKinley placed a hand on Mrs Crowley's shoulder in a reassuring manner. His other hand planted the drained mug precariously on the square corner of the banister. He hushed his tones to show he appreciated the gravity of the situation. With a kiss on his crucifix, he crossed the landing to a closed door. Smoked billowed from underneath the cracks, and the stench of rotten eggs was unbearable. McKinley pushed his hand under his nose. Mrs Crowley saw the gesture and explained.

- Sulphur.
- Probably eggs. Most likely eggs.

Mrs Crowley opened the bedroom door to reveal a teenage girl strapped to the bed, staring to the ceiling with milky eyes, muttering unintelligible words.

- She's been speaking in tongues for days.
- That's teenagers for you. It's like a unique language. Speak up my child, what do you have to say?

The girl twisted her head suddenly, her dead eyes staring at McKinley. A malevolent grin spread across her face, splitting the cracked skin on her lips. Trickles of blood poured from her mouth, black as pitch. A scaly tongue emerged from her mouth and mopped up the fluid. A voice, guttural and echoing, emerged from her bloodied lips.

- Would you suck Jesus's cock, father?

- Well, child, I'm a servant of God. So, if he asked, I'd have to oblige. To be sure, I wouldn't be happy about it so.
- Daphne! That is no way to speak to a guest!
- Daphne isn't here, Mrs Crowley! Only we remain!
- Might I ask, child, who is 'we'?
- Cabal. We are Cabal. We are legion!

Daphne growled, which developed into a manic cackle. Mrs Crowley, tears welling in her eyes, turned her head away as her daughter belched vomit in a jet into the air. The steaming ichor rose around four feet before splashing back down on her face and shoulders, eliciting fresh peals of laughter. Mrs Crowley closed the bedroom door, struggling to hold off sobs. Her eyes turned to Father McKinley pleadingly.

- What do you think? Can you... perform an exorcism?
- I don't think that's necessary. This might come as a shock to you, but I'm not sure she's possessed.
- What? What do you mean?
- I think your daughter is just mental.
- No! How can you say that after what you've seen? I want to speak to the cardinal!
- Now, hold on just a minute there, Karen. Today is only a consultation. We will have more time to figure out exactly how insane she is later.
- She isn't insane! Her eternal soul is in peril!
- Well, that's where we will just have to agree to disagree.

- How about you perform an exorcism today and prove me wrong that way?
- You see, I would, but I don't have any holy water with me. The words on their own, if it is demons from the pits of hell -and I'm not saying it is! She's definitely mental. I'm making that clear. If it is demons, then the words… well, they only piss 'em off. It's the holy water that is the key.
- Go back to the church and get some!
- Now that doesn't work. You see, proper holy water, the good stuff, only comes from the Vatican. And with Brexit, our shipments have been delayed. We tried saying prayers over some Evian, but that doesn't work. We should have some more by Tuesday week if that's OK.
- She could be dead by then!

Booming laughter could be heard through the closed door. A rhythmic banging started, growing in intensity. Daphne/ Cabal's voice permeated through the air.

- Fraud! Not even a real priest!
- Hush your gums you loony little cow!
- Father! Possessed or not, that is still my daughter!

Mrs Crowley paused for a second, as the words from beyond the door sank in. She placed her hands on her hips and probed Father McKinley.

- Is that true? Are you not a priest?

Father McKinley angrily grabbed his dog collar and pointed towards it.

- What der frig is this? They don't just give these out to anyone!
- I could get one from a fancy-dress shop!
- Not with this...Vatican seal of authenticity!

He tugged and twisted the dog-collar to show a barely visible seal. Mrs Crowley nodded, more in resignation than agreement. Satisfied, McKinley smoothed his collar, jutting out a defiant jaw. Daphne's voice bellowed.

- He's talking out of his arse!
- Mrs Crowley, you know what kids are like. Saying anything to get their own way.
- Or demons being deceptive.
- Ha-ha! Yes, maybe! But no, probably not demons. Just your crazy offspring.

McKinley took a step back, his elbow colliding with the mug, causing it to crash to the hallway below. The sound of the mug smashing startled Mrs Crowley.

- Did you just drop my mug?

She asked for reassurance. None came.

- Lord, no! I...
- What?
- I think...
- What?

McKinley gulped; his eyes widened as he whispered.

- I think you might have a poltergeist!

Like One Star.

By Grace King.

I answer to all,

even royalty,

but my praise goes to Rodents,

who assist me adoringly;

Red stained fingers abuse me;

Life says my vengeance,

on killers,

doesn't help my cause;

But our future plans are ruined;

I rage,

making silence;

She advises I steal teeth and other chores;

I bring out the best, the height of happiness,

but I can highlight the worst,

everything's exposed in my light;

I teach them to try;

I'm what makes them survive;

Death and I are a cycle but some,

fall asleep at the wheel;

When they oppress inner children, it's me that they kill;

My worst clients excuse all the work that I do;

Some run from my gifts after asking for help,

Teenagers need me but that's not why they seek me;

I give them the tools to create a good home;

Some adults can't sense me on their uninteresting days;

Invisible people waste what I sow;

My lover asks me to change up their ways;

My lover will attest that I'm a tough coach;

Maybe I'm too soft;

They should have some more faith;

No one is more my favourite,

than the content elderly,

Of my long acquaintance;

When one such perished,

we came to meet;

Lots in common,

we shared in our grief;

We'd been loving and hating,

hoarding each of our powers;

Then realised,

the world,

replicated our model;

She dropped her defences,

He swept me up from below;

We fell in love,

now we share all our goals;

I'm usually in trance when Death,

comes through the door;

I'm building new skin for critters,

that devour my warmth;

I'm waiting for Death to make what they've got fail;

I burst with excitement at the final details;

I love watching Life,

as she constructs from my work;

She weaves,

wades and ruptures,

my cold, opaque

murk;

I feel I'm my best,

when I'm,

around her;

Death circles in front,

and sits on the floor;

His hands hold my waist;

He strokes my long hair;

Dragon scales get shredded, as our lips beg for more;

We make sweet free will, as we shine like one star;

Let's put everything on hold;

You're my prisoner,

my rebel,

My dear, you must go;

Why can't they thrive,

without glass houses and pebbles?

my charm,

my woe?

Let's make Winter,

the new Summer;

A test,

for the damnedest,

Of souls;

I'm too hot for big jumpers,

so honey, it's a no;

I know you're romantic,

and you keep Mother clean,

but darling, I can't work,

if we stay in the sheets;

Spring needs to come and I need to breathe;

Stop crowding me, but PROMISE you'll watch all that I
achieve;

Of course;

As long as my name's,

spoken hoarse,

at the height of fame,

in your award,

winning speech;

It's true, we free each other,

from mindless consumption,

when we find that we're trapped,

in a recyclable dungeon;

One day we'll be joined;

I dream of the date;

No pain, no time;

Your souls have good fates.

The Headless Angel of Cleethorpes.

By

Oliver Gammon.

Marlow was wondering how it had come to this. He had been wondering this for quite some time. Well, for a year to be precise and he'd plenty of time to do so. Especially now that he was the head of a cursed statue, but this was not just any cursed statue. This statue through local folklore and legend was known as the headless angel of Cleethorpes. It wasn't so headless now, but we will get to that in due course. During Marlow's recalling of events, he wished it hadn't ended in such a messy way. But now that he was caught in the eternal limbo between life and death, he had plenty of time to replay the events of a year ago and wish it had ended in not such a gruesome fashion. As it began to get dark in the Cleethorpes graveyard (where else would a cursed statue reside and what better place for Marlow's tale to take place?), Marlow began to fully recall the details of that night in his mind's eye, it just happened to be that this eventful evening one year ago, just happened to be the most frightful night of the year, Halloween.

The three friends where walking through Cleethorpes graveyard one night as they usually did on

Halloween. As they had gone beyond the age of asking strangers for sweets. They now much preferred egging people's houses. Or rather, at least two of them did. The other member of the threesome did so reluctantly. Oscar wasn't as wild as his namesake, but he wanted to be part of the gang and would do these things to fit in. But since leaving school and now at the local college he'd come out of his shell somewhat. For the other member of the trio, he had always been the cool and calm one and likeable by all who met him, his name was Wesley. He had a nickname that he rather people used, and it just came to stick over time. If you went walking through Cleethorpes, from its sea front to its high street you would see this nickname sprayed on its walls. That name was Wezlo and it had become an in joke with his friends and school chums, as no one apart from them knew who this mysterious figure was. Now we get to the third of the trio and shall we say he's a bit rough around the edges. His name (as I've sure you have guessed by now) was Marlow. He could be a little bit crazy. Well, when you've used a bb gun illegally and the police have said you can go free with no charges, but you will have to take a mental health test instead, saying he's crazy was putting it lightly. He'd calmed down by now, but he still liked to live on the wild side. That being the reason they were now at the graveyard.

The three friends were all the same age of 17 so even though nearly being adults still liked the mystery allure and scare factor of Halloween. They had all heard of the legends of the headless angel. Wesley had teased Oscar enough about it in school and on their many walks home from their secondary school through the graveyard (as there was a path for cars and bikes and people that ran straight through it). It was on this very path in the dark that the three friends now found themselves, staring at the headless angel of Cleethorpes. "Well get on with it, Oscar! Throw the stones at it then, we ain't got all night," shouted Marlow. "OK nob, I'll do it now. Hold your horses!" replied Oscar. These two had never seen eye to eye. Marlow had been more Wesley friend than Oscars. They had been brought together more through Wesley, but an uneasy friendship between the two had settled in. Wesley still had to occasionally get in the middle of the two, just as he was doing now. "Hey, you two, chill. We know what we got to do, so just get on with it ok? Good!" So, Oscar through three stones one after the other, through the bars of the graveyard gate at the neck of the angel, where its head had once been again centuries ago. The they began to chant the words headless repeatedly. They'd all heard the legends of the ritual to get the statue to speak. They all thought it was just a stupid urban legend but that all changed in a heartbeat when they heard it wail and shout, "Who dares disturb my eternal slumber." The three friends did not know if to run, have a heart attack, or shit themselves. Or all three things at once.

The three friends did none of these things. They were just stuck and frozen to the spot in disbelief and listening to the statue speaking (well rambling to them). "You men are all the same, be it the 18th ,20th century or this god-awful century. You're all the same. Men are the reason I'm in this god-awful state I've been in for the last 200 years. "Excuse me your lady we're not all the same. If you tell us your problem maybe we can help you." where the courage came from, Oscar had no idea, but he'd just said the first thing that had popped into his traumatised head. "What can you men, children, do for me? Only by returning my head can the curse be broken, and I will finally find peace in God's kingdom." Well, the friends didn't know what to say, other than Marlow. It was a poor choice of words. "Fuck this and fuck you, you freak, this ain't our problem." "You've done it now gobshite, we're in for it now or should I say, you are!" replied Wesley in his normal and calm manner, even in such a bizarre and freakish situation as the trio now found themselves in. There was a massive and unusual silence, even for this ungodly time at night and in a graveyard of all places. Then a shriek and laugher like banshees from hell, brought all three friends to their knees. Once the sound had ceased and the trio ears had stopped ringing the statue spoke again but with more evil intent. "Looks like you have helped me. Well, your friend has, without knowing as the curse has passed onto him. And unless your foolish friend can return my head by dawn. Let's just put it in language your foul-mouthed friend can understand, he's fucked!" Then another ungodly sound came from the headless angel, it was the laughter off the eternally, and soon to be, damned. It now starting to dawn on Marlow that he was soon to join that very exclusive club. "Oh fuck!" was all he could manage to say. As he started to feel very sick, and he's legs began to feel like jelly and he

43

wished he was anywhere but here, at this very moment in time. "Well fucked indeed" said Wesley and Oscar at the same time, but it must be said, Oscar said it with more relish and glee than Wesley.

Once the hopelessness had left Marlow's mind. His normal quick wit returned, and he decided on a course of action. "Right Oscar, nowt for it will have to use your car and as for you freak features, where is your head then?" The statue replied to them this time with a sparkle of evil in her voice. "My child, it's not that simple there are four pieces you see. About 50 years or so I think, my head was smashed by children such as yourself. And for some reason the magic behind the curse scattered around the surrounding area. In other words, you best get on with it." The confidence that Marlow had shown earlier was utterly crushed by the angel's word, and it seemed to notice this immediately. "Don't despair child, not all is lost. Even though that same magic is a bizarre and confusing thing, it does have its advantages. Through some psychic link as your modern scientist would describe it, I can see through those pieces and still have a physical link to those pieces as well. I can even hear things that are said by people in those locations. I have a good modern knowledge of those places and their names have changed much since my death 200 years ago, of course. So, the first piece can be found in Weelsby Woods in the witches' circle. The second is at an abandoned military base where there are huge satellite dishes or some modern nonsense. The third is not far from the second location, in a shaft that goes down into a military bunker and the final

44

piece is around the area outside of the abandoned theme park called Pleasure Island." The trio took all this in, and it was Wesley who broke the silence in his normal cool and calm manner. "Best get on with then haven't we. You get your car Oscar and meet me and Marlow back at my place." As quick as that the trio where off into the night to try and stop Marlow losing his head, literally.

So, our misfortunate trio where soon on their way in Oscar's not so impressive Ford Focus. Oscar was not too happy about it. "My parents are gonna kill me!" "They won't even know will they and you're not the one who's going to lose his fucking head so deal with it!" Marlow put an end to that argument. I won't bore you with all the details as it's the end of tale we've all come here for, but they soon arrived at, and braved the darkness of, the witches' circle. Where many years ago a poor youth had been taken and murdered, but all that happened there now was teens hung out there, getting high and very drunk. The head was still able to communicate with the trio, as the angel was now psychically linked to Marlow. So, they found it under the big oak right in the centre of the circle. The next one was easy to find as Wesley had been to the second location with his dad many times. The dishes where long gone but there was an abandoned bunker and it just happened to be there. So, two down two to go. There was only three hours till daybreak, so Oscar put the pedal to the metal (well as fast as you could in a fifteen-year-old Ford Focus. They were soon speeding down an unnamed county road and with the angel's and Wesley's knowledge, once more they found the third location and the first piece, with wax down the shaft and the entrance to the underground bunker. Now they only had one more piece to go. They'd completed their travels and soon approached the abandoned theme park Pleasure Island. They had to approach this more carefully as this was not some abandoned world war site. There were still night watchmen there, to keep away gangs of youths and other would-be trespassers. So, once again they got the piece, though they did have to run for their lives back to the car once the guard dogs where released (thanks to Oscar stamping loudly on a discarded can of Coke), but they were soon speeding down the Cleethorpes Sea Front and on their way to the Cleethorpes graveyard and in the nick of time, as sunrise was only thirty minutes away.

"Well, there you go then freak we've got all your pieces!" Marlow said proudly as he placed all the fragments before the headless angel. "Good for you, but unfortunately, I lied. Getting these pieces won't stop the curse. I won't go into detail about it, but the warlock who put the curse on me said they only way for the curse to be lifted is if I got a man to curse at me quite literally, as you did my young friend. In ten minutes, I will be free from this mortal realm and will have my peace at last. Oh, and I forgot to mention the curse affects any men who are with victim as well. Sorry to mention it now at this late hour but, one's mind does get funny after 200 years." Marlow could hardly believe what he was hearing, and no words left his mouth, just an animalistic scream of rage, disgust and utter despair. Both his friends tried to restrain him, but it was no good. Marlow ran screaming and raving and once he got to the bars, screaming at the angel like a man possessed. The other two must not have heard what the angel said straight away, as Oscar remembered that he and Wesley were cursed as well. "How do we break the curse for us, I'll do anything?" Oscar shouted at the angel. "You two can be saved if you take the life of the cursed one!" shouted the angel. "No problem then," replied Oscar". "You can't be serious", said Wesley as he pleaded with Oscar. "He's been a pain in my back side forever, Wesley. It's him or us and I'm not going to damned because of Marlow s pig-headedness ". So, without any warning, Oscar rushed up behind the still ranting Marlow, and with all his strength and pent up rage, of years of being Marlow s punching bag, he pushed Marlow's head and all straight into the bars. Due to all the many years of neglect on the part of the groundskeeper, there were many damaged parts of the fence. This one particular part was a gap just big enough for a human head and neck, and it'd never been repaired, and it just so happened to be the same spot where Oscar now pushed Marlow's head into. With one finally effort, Oscar pushed Marlow s head all the way through. Unfortunately for Marlow (or fortunately for Oscar), Marlow s head went in at just the wrong angle for a human head to survive and there was no turning back. With an almighty scream of pain and massive cracking noise, Marlow's neck was instantly broken. He just was stuck there and just stone-cold dead at an angle a human body was never meant to be.

"What have you done?" wailed Wesley, uncontrollably. "What needed to be done!" snapped Oscar. "You're free to go. Your friend will take my place now, or at least his head will, farewell!" shouted the angel with glee. Suddenly and without warning there was red flash of light and Marlow's body and head vanished without a trace. The headless angel was headless no more. As the light began to come over the horizon and the birds began to sing, the last two surviving friends of the trio, could not believe their eyes. Without any time to think, they did the only thing they could, they ran, and they never looked back again, or ever visited a graveyard for the rest of the natural lives. So as our tale comes to a head (do forgive the pun) and we return to the present, and to Marlow's recalling of the events of a year ago, and still in his eternal nightmare. I think it's fair to say, Marlow wishes he'd used he'd head a little bit more (pun intended this time and no forgiveness needed either) on that fateful and frightful evening. Well good night, whoever or whatever you are.

Hooked Hanable.

By

Theresa May King.

Shaking shambles shivering in the harsh winter wind, Shop shutters shut, adding to the gloomy graphite sky. Ocean waves washing away the previous day's joy on sands of precious golden grains. The sky rumbles with anger then lights up the world with a Crack of white coils tumbling to the ground. Oh, the rain on that day seemed to fill every crack in the pavement, every pothole. In the old dirt tracks outside our city, every corner of our land was packed to the brim with this rain that the flood sirens seemed to screech through the air making the world hold its breath. This day was named Terrible Tuesday. And yes, it was terrible. My city, Sphynx, had its worst winter storm in 50 years. Our houses were not prepared for such weather and most of our livelihoods were flooded, damaged, and ruined. The lightning hit our green lands that caused several bush fires damaging many farms and parks.

This wasn't the reason this particular Tuesday on the 5th of December 1979 was deemed terrible…. It was the fate of Priscilla, otherwise known as Prissy Campbell and Carlos McDonald, that everyone believed this Tuesday was terrible, but first … let me give you some backstory before our story begins.

Priscilla Campbell was 16 years old in 1979. Well-loved by her community and born into the wealthiest family in town. Therefore, making her the biggest brat alive. She was the youngest of 4 siblings; all boys, and her whole family ran the police department. Priscilla was classed as sweet and caring by her peers... blah blah blah... I saw her as the demon from hell out to ruin my life. Not that anyone cared. She was head cheerleader and loved to be the center of attention.

Carlos James McDonald was 17. And you guessed it on the football team. Loved by everyone...but me. He was the only child of the city's best Lawyer couple. Mr. and Mrs. James and Lilly McDonald. Prissy and Carlos had the perfect relationship. They could do no wrong. They volunteered at homeless shelters, fed the hungry, visited the blind etc., etc. I saw the actual people behind their bright smiling faces. How they argued and fell out, how toxic they were together. How they bullied, lied, and beat the less fortunate. But nobody talks about that side of them.

Who am I? You may be thinking... my name is Hanable. Just Hanable. In 1977 aged 15, I butchered my whole family with a hammer and an 18-inch fishing hook. They deserved it. It was quite a sight. I managed to splatter the crimson liquids over the walls, and some even went on the ceiling of my house, impressive right? I posed my mother and father, older sister and brother together to become the perfect happy family we should have been and took pictures. I was deemed insane. But how I see it ... I'm not the insane one. Everyone else is just blind.

Rain. All she could see was rain through the steamed-up window of her boyfriend's red Hudson Hornet. The dark scenery around her would light up only slightly as they passed by. Her scowl made it clear she was still angry after they argued about stupid little things like forgetting the umbrella and not packing the picnic." how can you take me on a picnic date, in the middle of nowhere without the picnic" she bursts out again, keeping quiet wasn't the way she liked to keep things. She was far too strong-willed for that.

"I'm sorry Prissy," Carlos sighed once again. "I was in a rush, and it will still be nice we can listen to music and... talk" Carlos tried to lighten the mood with no success. He was met with silence, and Prissy wasn't in the mood to talk.

The pitter-patter of the rain hitting the top of the car and windows, the whooshing of the bushes passing by, and the occasional bump as they pass over a pothole was their music for a long while until they stopped at their usual spot overlooking the city below them. Luckily the view was something to distract them. Thunder cracks, lightning snaps forking down onto the buildings below. Occasionally an area of light would go out as the flood water cut off the power in that neighborhood. The wood around their car seemed to howl in the wind, scattering what was left of the Autumn leaves. Their branches making them curl into bony finger-like limbs reaching out at you in the wind. What's left of the grass and shrubbery coil back at their presence, making way for the thick swirling fog to ripple in, creating a dark, haunting feeling. Far from romantic.

"I am sorry... how can I make it up to you?" Carlos purrs at Priscilla, wiggling his eyebrows. This gets a small amused smile out of the girl before she begins to laugh "stop...goofball," she squeaks, pushing his arm in the giggling school girl kind of way, making him laugh with her.

Their eyes focus on the view for a while before Prissy's hand finds the diel to turn on the radio. Her curly blonde locks falling over her shoulders, making her flick them behind her once again; her big blue eyes find her boyfriend when their song starts to play.

"What a coincidence" he grinned at her making her roll her eyes.

Carlos pulls her into him, wrapping his red football jacket around her shoulders for warmth, letting her head rest on his shoulders.

"We still going for ice cream?" she began looking up at him with her big blue eyes he just couldn't say no to.

"Of course," came his reply with a small kiss resting on her forehead.

While the love birds got to their final resting place, I had proceeded to escape the living hell that supposedly is now my home for the rest of my life... not that I mind. it was more than worth it.

I had escaped barefoot with only a thin black shirt and my black and green striped trousers they gave you when inducted into the Asylum. Not very flattering, but I suppose nobody was ever going to see you again, so it didn't matter.

Fortunately, the Asylum was only 3 miles away from lovers' cliff and growing up on a farm. That distance wasn't something impossible for me to cross in a matter of hours.

I knew this area well. I had followed Carlos up here with numerous other women Prissy had no idea even existed. Just watching them...waiting. Gathering my hate for their very soul. Poor Prissy, if she wasn't such a stuck-up know it all bitch, I might have found an ounce of sympathy for her somewhere out of the depth of my soul. But if that was the case, completing my revenge mission wouldn't be as easy.

The rain stung my skin as I arrived at Lovers cliff. It was coming down hard; I didn't suppose they could see much, so I didn't see the point of coming out. surely a movie at home would be better...but then I remembered this is Carlos we are speaking about and any opportunity to flaunt his manhood at unsuspecting girls he will jump at it like a dog to a bone. I knew it was them before I could even see Carlos's car. Their arguing blared out of the metal box they called a car, and then I got a glimpse of red rushing through the trees, like a target painted on their backs. Instinctively my body follows them, and my brain zones in, ready to catch its prey. My mind was filled with a dark swirling fog covering any kind of doubt or insecurities I may have had. I was ready. They were going to die tonight, and nothing was going to stop me.

The couple sat in their favourite spot. Cuddling, but as you can assume...cuddling turns to kissing, and kissing turns to.... well... you get the idea. That's until Carlos innocently cries out another girl's name. And that was it. A fit of yelling comes from the girl under him; a few blows to his chest make him get up. The short teenage girl flings herself out of the car, slamming the door behind him." I knew it!" she shrieked as he chased after her. " No! it's not what it looks like!" Carlos tried to reassure, but yet again, Prissy wasn't having any of it. Their arguing gets louder and louder to the point where neither can hear the radio turn to static for a moment before an emergency announcement replaces the music.

"Urgent news. The Hooked Hanable, now 17 years of age, had escaped the lunatic Asylum several hours ago. If seen do not approach. According to wardens at brandy brook Asylum, he is very dangerous with violent tendencies. If seen, report to your nearest police station, stay home, lock your windows and doors and wait for updates. this is Amanda Lovett from Sphynx news signing off."

My heart dropped. The sound of the name they had given me after I murdered my family never sat right with me. I only slit my father's neck everyone else had a hammer to the head, so I don't know why they thought it was an appropriate name to give me. But at that moment, the realization dawned on me. I didn't have long to kill them, maybe an hour or two tops. I had to get working. Luckily, they were both out of the car. Do I just run in there and take my chances? Or should I go find where I last left my fishing hook and play the mind games?

I voted for the latter. Carlos was bigger and stronger than me and, without some sort of weapon id not stand a chance. Besides, frightened humans are easier targets, and my favorite games were mind games.

Unfortunately, neither Carlos nor Prissy heard this as their arguing was so loud, they drowned out the announcement.

"Please. just let's get back into the car and go for some ice cream so I can take you home," Carlos suggested holding out his hands in defeat. " no... I'm walking," Prissy insisted, pulling the strap of her lemon knee-high dress back onto her shoulder. Her pin curls going flat from the rain and the thin cloth of her dress sticking to her body. She turns stubbornly, walking down the dark road away from him. Prissy continued to walk, but Carlos didn't follow. His arm was thrown up into the air as he walked back to his car. She knew he'd eventually come to find her. He always did. The rain hit her skin and tumbled down her arms, leaving a cold chill behind. Her hair was now dark brown and sopping. Her dress was almost see-through as it was that wet. she was cold and angry and hungry. Her tiny kitten-heeled shoes clip-clopped against the gravel road. It echoed into the woodland around her. a thin fog spiraled around her feet, and all animals were silent. She was alone with her thoughts. Her trembling hands move to find her bag and find it wasn't around her shoulder like she thought it was.

A frustrated sigh escaped her lips as she walked back towards the car.

This was almost playing out like a bad horror movie. Perfectly timed too. Now Carlos was alone; all I had to do was lore him out into the woods and slit his throat without causing too much noise, so I didn't alert Perfect Priscilla of my location. Simple enough, right? Wrong. During the two years, I had been locked away, Carlos had become even more insufferable than he already was. His ego had grown twice the size of him. When he got a glimpse of me in the woods before he got into his car, his fragile manhood got in the way. He just had to call me out. He totally did the "who's there. What do you want" thing that all the egotistical male characters in horror movies do just before they die.

What an idiot. So out he trots, swaggering into the woods, trying to make himself look as big as possible, but in reality, it looks like he wet himself and was trying to not let the damp cloth touch his skin. I, however, dash from one tree to the next, drawing him further and further into the woodland. The fog that had rolled in about ten minutes before, swirling around our feet, making my figure seem almost ghostly. Not that my almost white complexion and blonde curly locks helped that much. I finally got to the place where I had left my hook. And luckily, it was still there. To be honest, I was starting to think someone would have found it and dug it up by now, but I suppose nobody knew I used to hide out here waiting for the perfect moment to slash open Carlos's throat.

Well, my time had come. Here I am, hiding behind a tree, the dim-witted teen stomping up to me, shouting like the idiot he is. Then the sky is littered with tiny droplets of red as my fishing hook slides through his throat like butter. The surprised look on his face forever pinned there as I watched the light leave his eyes and the blood gush down his neck. The thrill I felt as his warm blood went cold against my skin. The smell of pennies filling my nostrils, hyping me up like some sort of drug. I was ready. Next Perfect Priscilla. I head back to the car after setting up Carlos's body to be found later. A grin had formed on my face. This was the most fun I've had in ages! And it was going to get better. Priscilla was always a cry baby, and toying with her is my favorite part of this whole story!

It seemed quiet. The music still playing, but no sign of Carlos. Prissy rolled her eyes at this and flung open the car door. Picking up her small purse from the passenger seat. That's when she heard it, a low... cackle from the bushes. As she turned towards the noise, it stopped. The sound of the radio flooded her ears once more. Frowning, she turned back round to turn off the radio, and again the low cackle started. Priscilla turned quickly. The laughing stopped instantaneously. " Carlos...." her voice came in more of a frightened squeak than usual. She was met with silence. The fog seemed to thicken around her feet as the rain began to stop. " Carlos, this isn't funny..." again silence. Not even a bird.frowning, she loops the strap of her bag over her shoulder and closes the door. " Priscilllaaaa" came a breathy sing-song voice from the wood. " Carlos, stop; it isn't funny!" Prissy squeaked and slowly moved towards the bushes. A crunch of leaves and a shifting of a body came, so I couldn't be seen. " Carlos, come out! I want to go home," she demanded, crossing her arms looking into the wood. Not that she could see much, but it didn't matter as, from a nearby tree, something shimmered from the beams of the car's headlights. Slowly walking towards it, she finds Carlos's jacket ripped and torn up and a fishing hook dripping with blood hanging off a branch. Her dainty hands shake as she takes his jacket off the branch, I had hung it on. Her eyes dart around the vegetation hoping this all was a bad dream. Her eyes had grown big, and a child-like expression had appeared on her face. Pure fear. perfect. "Carlos? Carlos!" she called out into the silence. But her stomach had already dropped, and she must have felt my presence nearby because she started to retreat back towards the car, her pace going from a walk to a run in a matter of minutes.

Her breath caught in her throat, and the hairs on the back of her neck stood on end. "Prisssssyyyy" came from behind her. a breathy sing-song whisper that sends chills down her spine. She drops the jacket, and her hands' fumble at the handle of the car; before pulling the door open, she jumps in, closing it and locking it. Her breathing was rapid and heart pounding. The fog getting thicker around the car, making it harder to see.

"CRACK" lightning strikes the sky, illuminating a figure in the woods, my figure. This wasn't my plan, but it seemed to work well. She seemed to almost recognize it. tall, slim, ghostly pale features but blue eyes that seem to stare directly into her soul. "Priscillaaa," his voice came again, and the rumble of thunder overhead drowns me out. " Prissy, let me in."

Tears start to tumble down her face. Panic rising from the pit of her stomach. Hands trembling as she holds them as close to her as possible.

Everything goes quiet, and she frantically tries to see me through the fog.

"CRACK" another burst of lightning fills the sky showing her that I am no longer in the wood. The thunder rumbles, and everything is quiet apart from Priscilla's little terrified sobs. The car then shakes, sending a shriek of fear through Prissy's lips. Then silence again. she looks through all the windows but sees nothing.

The silence was unnerving. Till my god-awful cackle fills the air much, much closer now. " Leave me alone!!" she screamed out in hopes that I would just go away. I didn't. A loud cackle came, then " let me in" the sing-song tone was one you would use to a child who is being stubborn. " NO, go away" she screamed again. This wasn't the reply I wanted with a deep gurgling growl that bubbled up from the pit of my soul, anger filling me. I was running out of time. I shook the car from side to side, making it hard for Priscilla to keep upright. Then, "BANG! " The windscreen caves in towards her cracking as the beaten body of Carlos lands in a contorted position, bones bent the wrong way, body oozing blood. His face warped with fear, eyes open but void of life, a large gash from one ear to the other covered his neck. The boy lying ridged on the bonnet of the car. This was harder to do than it looked. Thank God she never looked up. I had fortunately found some rope in his car bonnet as I was running back. The idea struck me as an excellent way to create a distraction or terrify the girl more than I already had... which I was correct. It did frighten her. This was all going too well. But it was almost over, and my desperation for a kill was curdling in my stomach like sour milk.

It takes a few moments to process before a scream falls out of the girl. Her scream was full of fear and anguish, and she shook with the force of it. Her eyes tearing up, and fear propels her out of the car into the woods. Perfect! The cackle follows her though the deeper and further she goes, the more lost she becomes, the closer the laugh.

A scraping to metal against wood, the cracking of leaves under her heeled shoes, the laugh that will haunt her dreams follows her with no escape.

Panting, she stops at a tree. Catching her breath, sobbing. Trying to figure out her surroundings. But that's when she saw me. Up close this time. My face grinning like a Chesher cat, enjoying the chase, hair curly blonde like the angels depicted in paintings, skin white like snow speckled with red splatters of blood and a silver rusted hook dripping with the remains of Carlos. Recognition on her face appeared immediately as she began begging for her life. Like music to my ears. How I've waited so long for this day. And it sure has been an adventure!

"Leave me alone! Please." she sobbed at me, making me laugh, showing my teeth which, I had sharpened into triangles, like a shark's grin. " Perfect pretty Priscilla....don't cry," I cooed at her like I was comforting a child. A proud sinister grin forming on my face once again. " don't cry," I repeated, " SCREAM!" I moved with such speed it caught Prissy off guard. An animalistic scream envelops her as my beautiful face fills her vision. A searing pain fills her body to the point her world turns black forever.

I had finally caught revenge. My body washed over with an intoxicating sense of relief, only making me want more and more of this relief I felt. There is no way to describe the drugged-like feeling you get after you kill somebody. It's addictive, and I wanted more. But first, I had to escape leaving my kills to be found later on. With the police hot on my tail, I went into hiding for a week. The last thing I remember before I was caught was the news report about their deaths which filled me with glee and anger all at the same time. This is where our story ends for you. But for me, it isn't over.

"Priscilla Campbell and Carlos McDonald are the identities of the couple found dead Tuesday night on the lover's cliff. Their funerals will take place tomorrow with a candle-lit Vigil to be held at brandy brook high school that evening at 7pm. The suspect of the crime is Hooked Hanable, who is still on the loose. Any information about the couple or Hooked Hanable should come forward to the police. If you see Hooked Hanable, do not approach. Get as far away as possible and report him to the police. this is Amanda Lovett from Sphynx news signing out."

After Compline.

By

Mark Sandford.

The Lord bless us and keep us, Amen". As is tradition, the Parishioners leave the church in silence and apart from the bang of the North door on its hinges, due to an alignment issue, the Church settles once more into silence and a comforting sense of air as I go about tidying up, after Compline. Dousing the large candles in the candle holders on the Altar I get a feeling of satisfaction and that a prayer of thanksgiving would be appropriate on this All-Hallows' eve. I'd just finished genuflecting when a slow hand clap came from the back of the church. Which was a bit startling as I thought I was alone

- Well done boy! That was a lot better than the way you handled the Brexit guy*. I know it's been a long time but hey, you're much better than the last time.

Boy? Boy?! He called me boy! I'm 64 for God's sake. Who is he?

- Yes, who are you and what are you doing here? I thought everyone...
- Had gone, he interrupted. Yes well there you are and here I am. The name is John. JP to my mates, my

God is this real gold? And he then lifted one of the candle holders and tipped it upside down looking for a hallmark. The candle clattered on the floor as I snatched it back off him saying

- I'll have that back if you don't mind, you'll get oil all over the place

And I returned the candle and holder to its rightful place.

- Oil? In my day we had proper candles. Do you still Chuck the old incense about? I loathed the stuff, made me sneeze.
- No, we don't and if it's alright with you I think you'd better go. I want to lock up and go home.
- Not going anywhere mate. Not yet anyways. You go on ahead and finish up here, I'll just hang around for a bit, perhaps put me hands together, you know how it is.

So, I finished off putting Bibles and prayer books away in the vestry, and to sign the register when I caught in the corner of my eye that the candles on the altar were lit. I'm sure I'd put them out but nevertheless I marched down the aisle of the church with the candle douser in hand and once again put the candles out. JP or whomever he was just knelt there at the altar. In fact, the air around him was noticeably colder than what it had been and for all in tense and purpose John or JP to his friends looked devoid of any life at all. I reached out to touch him, and immediately he came to life and shouted Boo! Which surprised me so much I fell over, tripping on the hem of my cassock.

-Oh, this is fun! What shall we do next, I wonder?

-Nothing

I said as I endeavoured to get to my feet. I marched back down to the vestry and shouted back to JP as he was well known by, that it was time to go home and if he didn't go soon, I would be calling for the police. By now I had started to take my robes off and I signed the register, when the sound of organ music came to my ears. I looked up into the organ loft, and sure enough there he was playing of all things Bach's Toccata and Fugue, and damn good as well. I couldn't say how he got into the organ loft, because he needed to walk past me to get there. I listened for a while then reached for my cell phone and dialled 999, only to realise that I couldn't get a signal. So, I figured the best thing to do was go outside. Only I couldn't open the door. I wasn't locked in, this much I knew but it seemed to be stuck.

- Leaving so soon? Come on I'm just getting warmed up!

The candles on the Altar suddenly burst into flames, but they were shooting flames three feet into the air in a pulsating fashion. Also, the Altar cross which was solid brass and heavy, floated in mid-air and was swivelling. Frightened, I pulled on the Church door as hard as I could, just as hymn books were flying out of the store cupboard and the lights were flickering on and off.

The door gave way suddenly, as a deep guttural voice, which seemed to come from everywhere said GET OUT! And the door flew open.

I ran down the churchyard and tripped on something and to stop myself from flying, I held onto a gravestone. In the moonlight I was able to read the inscription on the gravestone. It read:

Here Lies Reverend John P Harvey

Born 1804 Died 1860

Rest in Peace

I looked back at the church Which looked like there was a disco happening inside it and ran as fast as I could. I never went back....

The Doll Room.

By

Victoria Hydes.

Isla stared up at the weathered wooden door before her, back down at her phone's Google Maps pin, and up at the door again. Yes, this was definitely the place. She couldn't quite recall where her interest in peculiar architecture first came from, but once she'd put out the feelers for a new column for her online lifestyle blog focusing on showcasing the coolest and quirkiest homes the country had to offer she'd received a surprising amount of interest and support. Of course, she rarely heard from the more ordinary people who she could only assume held similar reservations to her about a letting stranger in to report on and judge their personal home. This worked for her though, as it freed up her inbox specially for only the most intriguing of clients.

It was one of these messages that had brought her here, to this rundown townhouse that so far looked disappointingly non-descript. She took a deep breath and raised her fist, knocking purposefully on the door. A few moments passed and she was about to try again when a distant creaking sounded from the other side, no doubt some kind of neglected floorboard in-keeping with the building's rustic exterior. She braced herself as the door eased open and she was met by a tall and slender man with shaggy dyed-white hair, broad-rimmed square glasses and a slightly frayed gingham apron unflatteringly caked in the remnants of whatever he'd just been attempting to cook. So much for first impressions.

"Hi there," she eventually breathed, plastering on her best fake smile and extending her hand in greeting, trying desperately to distract herself from his unconventional presentation and whatever that overwhelming scent was.

"I assume you're here for the tour, yes?" he grinned, removing his apron and tossing it effortlessly aside to the dusty floor below.

"That's right, Isla Rosewood."

"Well, the pleasure's all mine, Isla Rosewood. You can call me George. Shall we?"

He was already on the move before Isla even had a chance to respond. Fumbling around in her worn leather satchel for her notepad and camera she hurried awkwardly after him, almost tripping over an unruly stack of discarded books on the way. So far, nothing about this place matched the description she'd been given in the slightest, but she figured she'd give him the benefit of the doubt for now, at least until she'd seen some more of it.

Her disappointment continued as she took in one painstakingly ordinary room after another. To be fair, the house did come across more like one of those stately show homes owned by the National Trust than the kind of place the average person would live, but that didn't change the fact that it was nothing she hadn't seen before. Maybe it was because her last stop had featured a series of elaborate tunnels to get around, painted with all the colours of the rainbow, but this one just seemed exceptionally dull and she found herself distracted from his droning by thoughts of ways she could spin the piece to make it work.

Just as she was about to suggest they cut the tour short during a brief period of quiet, she finally spotted something that piqued her interest. Sensing her hesitation, George stopped and smiled his crooked smile. Before them stood a door brandishing a crudely hand-carved sign with the words 'The Doll Room' etched into its grain. Either side stood a small pedestal housing an immaculately kept porcelain doll, faced towards it and posed with outstretched arms, almost as though luring passers-by towards the entrance somehow.

"The Doll Room?" she frowned. "You like to collect dolls?"

"Oh yes, it's my most favourite pastime," he enthused, his eyes lighting up like those of a child on Christmas morning. "This room's especially important to me. This is where I put all my new dolls before I find a proper place for them. It's like nothing else you've seen today, I assure you."

She watched him for a few moments through narrowed eyes, picking up on his excitement almost immediately. She had to admit, it did sound a little creepy, but maybe, just maybe, this could be the room to save the article and make her journey there worthwhile after all.

"After you," he continued, stepping back with open arms to allow her passage to investigate for herself. "Oh, and I'll take your things for a moment, just to be on the safe side."

She wandered in with caution, reminding herself not to touch anything she might accidentally damage; only to her surprise there wasn't anything there to damage. In fact, there wasn't a single doll in sight in the entire space, just an ornate floor-length mirror standing proudly in the middle of the dimly-lit room. Her attention was drawn to the small notecard sitting atop a side table by the mirror, which she picked up and turned over in her hand a couple of times, her heart rate accelerating as she began to wonder what was really going on. She turned to ask where the dolls were just in time to see the door slamming closed in her face with a deafening crash that echoed through the new air of silence that surrounded her, followed soon after by the turning of a key in the rusty old lock.

"Hey!" she called out to nobody in particular. "What's going on?"

No response.

Pivoting swiftly back towards the mirror she gazed at her paler-than-usual reflection for a few seconds, before finally straining to read exactly what was written on the card, a cold sweat running down the back of her neck as her eyes travelled across its surface, letter by letter.

'Welcome to your new home, my Doll.'

Little Red.

By

Rebekah Richards.

In a small town on the edge of some woods, legend had heard a tale of a girl only known as 'Red Riding Hood'; more often than not with the word 'little' in front of this to imply some form of innocence. She was not, as fairy tales dictate however, a sweet innocent little girl who had strayed from the path through the woods and had a scuffle with a wolf. That is merely just a tale told to children by parents trying to teach them how to behave and do as they are told, for fear of something worse. No, this 'Red Riding Hood' of legend was not a friendly person at all and such was the horror of her tale that her name was forbidden to be spoken in the town, both her name and the title she had earned. So forbidden was the mention of her that she disappeared into the accusation of a myth. I can, however, attest to the fact she exists. I also know you never should want to meet her either in the deep dark woods that she is supposed to reside in, not in the brightly lit town in broad daylight and certainly not in any surrounding villages or the countryside.

How come, you may ask no one else testified to her existence? Well you see, I found out the hard way. In order to prove her existence one must first summon her by calling out to her 3 times. "Little Red, Little Re- ..." well you get the idea. I don't even want to write it a 3rd time in case I summon her from the depths of hell. Getting her to appear is easy, banishing her from whence she came is nigh on impossible. I am uncertain I have the strength to rid me of her again. You might as well open Pandora's Box than to summon her; it would be easier to deal with the aftermath. For the sake of ensuring I don't summon her again we shall just call her 'Red'.

How did it come about that I had summoned her, you ask? I was young, stupid, naive and had succumbed to the temptation of a dare. I only hope that this account reaches the news before these dares trend and go viral all over the world; finding her to banish her again would be so much harder in a big city. Who is 'Red' you ask? Well she is the devil's daughter or as she was known more commonly in the olden days, Lilith, as named after her mother, yet she is much more deadly.

I was 15 when I first encountered Red. It was at my friend's sleepover and we were having a good old fashioned game of truth or dare. I chose my favourite; a dare. Unfortunately for my friends it was the worst decision of the night. I was never scared of going through with a dare; summoning Red at Madison's suggestion was the perfect one for me. No one thought I would do it; except for Laura perhaps. She knew me all too well. In hindsight, however I wish I hadn't. Had I chickened out perhaps Laura would have still been here today; the silver lining is that I am now able to warn others against repeating my mistake. It was sheer luck that I am able to tell you of my tale. Red doesn't usually leave any survivors once she has had her fun. I implore anyone reading this not to repeat my silly mistake; I would hate for anyone to lose someone close to them in the gruesome way I did.

It was unexpected the way Laura died and had I not seen it for myself I might have thought that it was some form of suicide. You see, Red likes to have fun with her victims first, a little demon possession, getting up to mischief using her victims as a host. She is clever though, she really gets inside her victims' heads so by the time anyone realises they have been possessed rather than just acting a little more mischievously it is too late. She has already had possession of them for too long by that time that they either start to come apart at the seams, almost literally, or in some cases explode. The human body can only hold Red within it for so long. With Laura, it looked like some form of self-mutilation, even my testimony to let the police know exactly what happened fell on deaf ears. They still ruled it as suicide, while in reality her flesh had literally torn itself apart forming huge gaping holes until she bled to death, bleeding from every orifice at the same time.

Laura had a cheeky personality and a very active imagination, so it was 3 weeks before everyone realised she wasn't playing along and Red had actually come when I called her. I had already grown suspicious before then and had started my research into Red in effort to try and save my best friend, but I was too late. Course after Laura died, the others soon followed; they knew it was coming but I was powerless to stop it. Red couldn't risk word getting out for fear of being banished. She hadn't banked on me finding out how to get rid of her that's for sure. She took Emily next, making her jump off a bridge, Amanda followed that; hit by a bus. I had managed to save Madison, somewhat. I stuck to her like glue after Amanda knowing that Red would have to try to take us both down together. That was when I banished her. Unfortunately Madison couldn't handle all she had witnessed and spiralled into madness, maybe it would have been kinder to have let her die than suffer the way she does.

My first encounter with Red was bad enough, especially when you consider I was only 15 at the time but over the years she has gotten worse. Looking back I feel now that Laura was the lucky one in her possession. For Laura, it started a couple of nights after the sleepover. She was staying over at my house while her dad had to go out of town for a business meeting; this was nothing new, she practically lived at mine half the year. Everything was normal until around 3am when she suddenly woke up screaming; she never had nightmares and couldn't even remember this the following morning. The next day at school she was cheekier in class than usual, back chatting to the teachers and simply playing the fool. Don't get me wrong we weren't angels at school but even she knew when to draw the line. At first I just thought she was trying to get attention with her dad being away as she sometimes would pull stunts to get them to ring him so he had to come back, but then it happened every day after that.

Laura carved her name into every table in the maths classroom with a compass one day, saying 'Beware Laura is here, say your prayers asshole'. Everyone thought that was funny, except for the teachers. The next day she drew the devil on every white board in the school with permanent marker with the name Lilith underneath. No one could see the connection between Red and Lilith at this point as it wasn't until later that I found out her true name. At lunchtimes she would run through the school corridors chanting for Red much to the humour of the other students; they thought it funny that she was taking the piss out of the whole thing, believing themselves that summoning Red was just a scary story or a good idea for a dare for sleepovers.

The following week she loosened the brackets that held the basketball hoops in place which made them come crashing to the ground; fortunately being the summer P.E mostly took place outside and so no one was in the gym that day. Each night she stayed at mine she would continue to wake at 3am screaming, laughing, crying or just standing in the corner of the room quietly rocking back and forth. I even woke up one night to find her crouched over me with a pair of scissors in her hand as she had been cutting my hair in her sleep. No one knew where it would end and it was starting to get creepy. The final straw for me was the day she decided to turn on every gas supply for the Bunsen burners in the chemistry lab and ran off laughing maniacally. If the teacher didn't smell the gas before turning on the lights in the lab, the whole school could have gone up. Laura was always a practical joker but would never do anything to endanger life. I knew for certain she wasn't just playing along. That was when I started my research. I only wish I took the practical jokes more seriously sooner, maybe then I could have saved her.

Since ridding me of Red after that I have encountered her several more times in my effort to stop people from repeating our mistake; you would think people would have learned by now. It has pretty much become a full-time job tracking her down every couple of years or so when word gets out about people behaving out of character. Just call me Debbie, the Demon Hunter, no seriously though, it is getting tiresome. In the past she has tried to avoid me like the plague knowing I know how to banish her but recently it feels like she has been seeking me out. I think she wants to kill me before I get chance to send her back to the underworld so that she can stay here and have her fun. That is why I am being extra careful to not call her 3 times. I am unsure what she would do if I called her to me again. You see Red must stay within close contact of the person who summoned her, at least initially. The more she possesses those around the one who called to her the stronger she gets and the chance of her taking over increases. It is said in legend that when she grows strong enough she would open the gates between here and the underworld and we would be overrun by demons. I am not willing to allow her to get strong enough to find out.

Over the years I have encountered stories of Red being responsible for a number of antics from simple practical jokes right up to school shootings. Her favourite appears to be to take possession long enough to send family and friends spiralling into madness before finishing off with having her victim commit suicide. Although the school shoot outs after we week or two of almost exemplary behaviour is becoming one her more popular methods lately. I blame the internet and the media for giving her this idea; there is too much negativity around these days. Don't even get me started on the kind of antics she likes to get up to if summoned on Halloween; those unfortunate souls don't even last the night. That is the one day of the year I can pretty much guarantee it will come up as a dare and if followed through I can also guarantee I would not be there in time to save one single soul who bears witness to the game. The only thing I cannot guarantee is how many innocent victims will be taken down in the process. I still get chills when I think about the year she was summoned by a teenage boy and his friends who decided one Halloween it would be fun to use their Ouija board. Demons and Ouija boards do not mix. This ended with the boy's younger brother playing host to Red and decapitating his entire family and the children at the party before writing 'L... Red' on his bedroom wall and finally jumping to his death.

When will people learn that these legends must have come from somewhere and that even chancing an encounter with anyone of these entities could lead to complete disaster? My most recent encounter with Red, I have to say, was definitely my worst. She is getting bolder in her antics; I genuinely believe that she does not care if people discover her identity. My main concern is that after each encounter she appears to be getting stronger. The more time she spends in our realm, the harder it is to banish her; pretty soon I don't think I will have the strength to do it on my own. She doesn't even appear to be as tied to her host as she previously was. If she becomes able to taking forms of her own I dread to think what she will do.

Her latest visit to our realm left me in no doubt that her freedom would be the end of ours. It started off mild; first she started with tying fireworks to a cat's tail in the middle of a family gathering. The children were distraught with what happened to the cat but no one suspected Philip, Red's latest host, and passed it off as kids from the neighbourhood playing some sick practical joke. After that Philip and his younger siblings took to cooking a rabbit for their dinner before Philip then revealed that they were in fact eating Bugsy, their pet rabbit. That was when people had started to suspect Philip was under some influence but with his age passed it off as some recreational influence. No one really suspects possession these days as religion takes more of a backseat in today's culture. If one doesn't believe in the existence of God or some God like figure, you can be certain that they also do not believe in the existence of Demons.

The final part of the visit was the one that nearly destroyed the town. No longer content possessing humans she took to tormenting the local zoo once her host, Philip, lost his life jumping in front of a train. No one knew she was even there until to zoo keeper went to feed the lions. The result of which left the local community in tatters as first the lions ate the zoo keeper and then escaped on a rampage. The giraffes became 3 headed beasts of destruction, pulling down power lines and traffic lights, attacking anyone who tried to stop them. This lead to multiple car crashes and failures in equipment at the power station due to the disruption in the power lines fortunately an explosion at the nuclear plant was narrowly avoided with the backup generator kicking into action. Red had seemingly managed to possess multiple entities at once, though to be honest I'm more or less entirely sure that she had help from her friends in the underworld. Even the innocent looking characters in the petting zoo such as the goats and guinea pig manage to claim some lives for their own. I will never know how I managed to remove all that chaos. I felt sure that even banishing her would have left some of her friends behind. You may wonder why this is my worst encounter and not the previous which led to decapitation. Well, simply put, decapitation is more friendly death than the mauling and mutilation the others suffered at the hands of zoo animals. The death count alone is enough to make it top of the list; Red had waited for a major reopening day of the zoo where a new attraction, the lions, were to be revealed which only meant more visitors than usual.

One consistent thing I have is that almost all my encounters have involved teenagers being responsible for summoning her with only one encounter being a group of adults who were trying to do a documentary on the subject. Unfortunately, any footage they did manage to get is corrupted, so I have no proof other than my word that she is not some fictional character and that doesn't seem enough for a lot of people. The major difficulty I face is sorting out the liars; it's all too easy to shift responsibility for your actions if you blame it on being possessed. It is for this very reason I am documenting my encounters with Red in the hopes that it will help to put a stop to these silly little school game, but also to educate those who find themselves accidentally doing so. There is only one way to get rid of Red and banish her back to where she came from.

You must draw a circle on the floor and line the circle with lit red candles. In the middle of the circle draw a 5-point star with a lit black candle on each point of the star. For this to work she must be there with you so placing an object belonging to the person who summoned her in the middle of the star, you will then need to call for her three times; the candles will then trap her there long enough for you to chant the following words.

"Oh unseen forces help me now with my plight

And banish this evil from my own sight

For whom I had once called forth to me

The true name of Lilith I give back to thee"

Repeat the chant until she completely fades from sight. It will work better if there are more people there to chant it together. It is often the case that I have to work alone as I am unable to save everyone who witnessed her arrival due to having to find out second hand where she is or people think I am completely bonkers and Red doesn't actually exist. I am hoping that by getting this information out there more people can be saved or better yet that people will stop summoning Little Red …

The Cottage.

By

Denise Light.

C'mon, let's go in."

"Don't want to."

"Are you scared?"

"Just don't see why you want to go inside."

"Well, we might see a ghost."

"Exactly."

"Well, if you don't want to go in you can stay here while I go and have a look."

And of course, because he said that, she ended up going with him.

The cottage had been there for over a hundred years, more like two hundred some people said. When the last occupier, old Mrs Marshall, had died, the solicitors had not been able to find out who inherited it so it had stayed unoccupied and unloved .

Joel had heard the rumours in the village, that it was because of the ghost that the cottage hadn't sold. He wanted to see the state of the building thinking that there was an opportunity to earn some money by advertising it as haunted.

Which was why he was here today. His girlfriend Lucy had come with him, reluctantly. She couldn't see the point in acquiring a ramshackle cottage. But Joel was always coming up with money-making ideas and this was the latest.

Joel opened the door with the key he'd got from the solicitors and went in. Lucy was right behind him. They both gasped. It was as though they had stepped back in time. The room didn't look as though it had been altered in the last 50 odd years.

They looked all over the cottage. Everywhere it was the same, the same as it would have looked 50 years before.

"This is perfect," said Joel. "And at the moment I don't think there's a ghost."

"What do you mean?" asked Lucy "at the moment."

"I think we could do up the outside and offer people a night or 2 in a haunted cottage."

"But it's not haunted!"

"No, but it will be'"

And so, Joel used up all his savings and bought the cottage, did it up outside, provided the necessary items for people to stay there and marketed it as a "haunted cottage".

What Lucy didn't know was that Joel had added some extra features, sounds and shakes and lights, to produce the right element of fear.

It proved to be a huge success. Joel was quite canny, producing just the right amount of ghostly features, depending on who was staying there. Sometimes he only created a few noises. Once he produced some ghostly smoke which was very successful.

Of course, Lucy still didn't know about the added features. Joel had early on decided that it would be his secret.

The first Halloween, however, proved to be a bit different. Two students from Oxford had booked the cottage for the night. Everything seemed just the same as usual. Joel had set things up so that the lights would flash and there would be a few ghostly noises.

But when the students brought the key back the next day they were so excited. They had seen a ghost! Joel frowned. "Which ghost?"

"Is there more than one?"

"We saw a girl, she must have been about 16, certainly younger than us. She looked very sad and held out her hand to us. When we went to hold her hand she just faded away."

Joel had to think very quickly. "You are so lucky. We don't know who she is and it is only rarely that anybody sees her."

Lucy had come up behind him and had heard everything that had been said. "We need to find out who she is so we can tell her story and attract more people to the cottage."

"Too right!"

Lucy managed to find out that the girl had been killed by a farm worker. She had been a servant to the owner of the cottage. The owner was a widow whose son used to come and visit. He became obsessed with the girl, Ann. One day he came to see his mother, but she had gone to visit a neighbour so the young man, Will, pestered Ann to give him a kiss. She refused and went to run out of the cottage to the neighbours but before she could get out of the door she fell and hit her head on the stone floor. Will was charged with murder but as it couldn't be proved conclusively he was freed.

"So, she's just asking for help" said Lucy "when she reaches out her hand."

Joel and Lucy produced a board which they put up inside the cottage which told Ann's story. The cottage continued to provide them with a healthy income. But it was only very rarely that anybody actually saw the ghost of Ann Barber. Joel never did tell Lucy about the added features!

Take a Walk With Me.

By

Bee Ashton.

Take a walk with me

Down to the tree

In my home at the bottom of the garden

Where I sit in despair

Pondering why life is unfair

And wondering when it will end

Will it end with a noose around my neck

The rope I did check

On the tree at the bottom of my garden

And when I stand

Will you hold my hand

As from this life I depart

You see he whispered to me

With sweet lies and deceit

And in his image I did terrible deeds

Georgia, sweet Georgia

Can you not see?

Only I am your one true friend

I held your hand

I let you stand

High above everyone else

For they weren't as special

As you, sweet Georgia

Now hurry, complete your task

One remains look, see, how he turns

To the tree at the bottom of your garden

He's removing the rope

See how he dismissed your hope

Quick, the rock do it quickly

Bash in his head

Lift the rock and-

NO

Oh

There is blood on my hands

They shake and they sag

As the rock tumbles to the ground

You sway on one spot

Turn and fall, you're now dead

And a smile reaches my lips

I am finally free

From their sweet lies and deceit

And with a laugh I dance with him

My one true friend

Who was there until the end

And will be with me forevermore.

The Scar.

By

Mike Nelson.

'm not the biggest fan of Halloween. Each year is a painful and horrid reminder of what happened to me. Everytime I look in the mirror, or when I'm getting changed at the gym. People would stop and stare, then ask me 'How did you get that scar on your chest?' I always lie and say 'Operation' the truth is I'm not hundred percent sure on how I got the scar. But since Halloween that year, I will never go camping again.

This story takes place a few years ago. My roommate Poppy and I were getting into the creepy spirit and Poppy was getting excited for twenty-first birthday which was also on Halloween. Every end of October since we all turned eighteen, we all went out and got drunk. But this year we wanted to do something different.

"Why don't we go camping this weekend?" I suggested.

"Camping Daisy?" Poppy said

"Well, it's Halloween, why don't we?" I suggested.

"Where?" Poppy asked.

I showed Poppy an online article on my laptop. She burst out laughing.

"Seriously?" Poppy gasped. "You don't believe that nonsense."

I didn't respond and closed my laptop and narrowed my eyes. I was slightly annoyed over my friend's sudden rude outburst.

"What, you don't believe in that paranormal shite?" Poppy asked.

"Well." I replied. "Remember what happened to the bar-girl?"

Poppy rolled her eyes and shook her head.

"Look, why don't we go and check out?" I asked again.

"No," Poppy snapped.

"Why scared?" I mocked.

Poppy clenched her fist clearly angered over my sudden insult and gave me a small death glare. I could tell her curiosity was getting the best of her and deep down she wanted to see if the 'story' was true.

"Fine." Poppy sighed. "But Heather and Lilly are coming as well."

"Fine." I said. "Anything else?"

"Erm." Poppy said. "If we don't see anything scary. You'll have to buy the rounds for the next month."

"Deal," I said. Whilst shaking Poppy's hand.

Saturday had arrived and the four of us had crammed into Poppy's small car. We drove down an overgrown road. The leaves had made the drive a little precarious, many small pot holes and ditches were cloaked in the Autumn foliage. We spent an hour driving up and down the same four roads, until Poppy stopped her car.

"Daisy?" Poppy asked in a confused tone. "Is that it?"

We all looked two our left and noticed a large open gate. It was made from silver and was decorated with Celtic symbols. We all looked at each other.

"Didn't we just drive past here?" Lilly asked.

I nodded, looked at my google map app and nothing. I wasn't scared but I was definitely confused. Poppy, showing no fear, just got in the car and entered the gate. We were in a cemetery. I once again checked my app and nothing. This cemetery wasn't on the map.

"This must be a new cemetery." I thought.

Until Heather shouted. "Hey look at that"

We all looked towards where Heather was pointing and my theory of this was a new cemetery was put to bed. Right at the back of the cemetery, barely visible was a pair of large iron doors, with no lock and slightly opened. Poppy's expression changed, she had slightly smirked and looked at the three of us.

"No way!" Heather shouted. "I'm not going in there."

"I'm not either!" Lilly snapped.

Me and Poppy looked at each other. We both knew we would be going in there. I took a huge sigh, then with Poppy's help pushed the door open. The first thing that hit us was the smell. Bizarrely, it was quite pleasant; it smelt like a strong rose perfume.

Leaving Heather and Lilly outside. Me and Poppy continued walking down a small narrow path. It was dark and cold. But the smell of roses got stronger. It quickly turned from pleasant to overpowering. The smell seemed to be coming from the end of the path, until we came across another door. Feeling a little braver we pushed open the second door only to find a small chapel.

It was decorated in marble, and had bright red rose bushes growing out the walls and floor. The aisle was also decorated in marble, but had small red jewels embedded in the rock. It looks like something from a gothic horror novel.

"What the fuck have we stumbled on?" Poppy asked.

"I don't know but....." I paused and noticed a large blood red curtain.

Poppy had also noticed the hanging rag. She gave me that same smirk as before and opened the curtain. The pleasant smell of roses had gone. In its place was the smell of rotting flesh and horse shite. The smell caused me to vomit.

"FUCK!" I gasped, as chunks of cornflakes and coffee poured out of my mouth. "How aren't you throwing-up Poppy?"

I looked up and Poppy was glaring at me, she wasn't laughing, she was shocked.

"You were right, look?" She gasped.

I swallowed the vomit and composed myself and followed Poppy's arm with my eyes. Then I saw it, standing there looking still, ancient and carved in the marble was a woman. No this must be the maiden.

"Is this her?" Poppy asked in a sceptical yet slightly worried tone. "Granted we've found her but now what?"

I pulled my phone out and checked out the legend. I narrowed my eyes and I felt like a bit of an idiot.

"We need to come back later during the night." I said. "That when she walks."

Poppy shook her head. Clearly, she was spooked, and was trying to stay brave.

"I leave this here." She said placing her phone on a nearby stand. "Then I will have video evidence."

I was a little shocked, she was going to leave her phone, but then she gave a reassuring smirk, and pulled out her actual phone.

"That's my old one," she said. "It's fully charged and has a battery-bank connected to it. Should last till tomorrow."

With our 'surveillance' ready we left the tomb and reunited with Heather and Lilly. Poppy had connected all our phones to the one left in the tomb. With night closing in we decided to set up a camp across from the cemetery gates. We spent the remaining hours of daylight taking photos and checking the surveillance and celebrating Poppy's birthday. Nothing happened so we decided to camp out in the car, well it beats having Halloweeners banging at the door, and we all fell asleep. Clearly exhaustion had gotten to us, so we decided to look at the video in the morning.

I was woken up by a chorus of church bells. This was strange. We hadn't heard any bells ringing since we got here. I was groggy, annoyed because the others were still asleep, and I needed to pee very badly. Not wanting to wake the others I slowly opened the boot of the car and went behind a large tree. As my hot piss warmed the cold Autumn floor, I checked my phone. The video had stopped.

"I bet she didn't fully charge the battery." I mumbled.

Naturally, I wanted to wake her up and tell her. But then I would have woken Heather and Lilly. I thought it was best just to leave them to sleep and besides I was feeling rather brave. A quick shake, because I had no toilet paper, great. Then I entered the cemetery alone.

As soon as I walked past the gates, everything seemed a little off. A fog had randomly appeared and everything was pin drop quiet. The only form of company I had was the sound of my footsteps walking along the gravel path. Then as I walked deeper into the homes of the dead. My footsteps gained an echo.

Every time I moved, it was if someone or something was moving. I stood in silence and tried to control my breath. After a couple of seconds, I heard, "THUD!" Is one of the girls playing a cruel trick on me? I slowly kept walking towards my destination, but the loud thuds wouldn't go away.

"Hello?" I shouted softly trying to sound brave. "Heather? Lilly? Poppy?"

No response. I took a deep breath and regained my nerves and entered the tomb and to where we left the phone and battery bank. As I suspected both items were dead. I shook my head in frustration and was about to leave but my curiosity had got to me again.

For my own reassurance I turned my phone towards the statue. Hoping that she was still there. My heart began to race, sweat dripped from my head, and my jaw dropped to the floor.

"She's...gone?" I muttered. "She fucking gone!"

Scared, I ran out of the tomb faster than a bolt of lighting. I was screaming louder than a siren as I ran across the gravel path and jumped over the odd grave. Suddenly, my body crashed into something. The impact had caused me to fall to my backside and my head was dripping with blood, it nearly knocked me out.

In my dazed state I slowly looked up, and I started breathing heavily.

"What the.... fuck?" I muttered. "It can't be!"

It was the maiden. The legend was true, she was walking, she was alive and I was in danger. The Maiden expression had changed from a peaceful praying woman. To someone demonic and angry. I scrambled to my feet, trying to make ground between me and the Maiden. She raised her hands and started chasing me.

I screamed as I ran into a nearby tree line. For a statue her agility was deceiving, as soon as I dived into a small bush, she had practically caught up with me. She slowly walked past and turned her head. The sound of marble on marble was like nails on a chalkboard. It was loud and made you shudder.

A few seconds felt like hours, as she stood in the middle of the open patch of woods. Suddenly, the bell started to ring. She turned towards the direction of the cemetery and walked back, still turning her head around. I'm guessing she wanted one shot to attack me.

I checked my phone, midnight. Has she returned back to the tomb? I didn't want to stay and find out. I composed myself, took a deep breath, then ran blindly back to the car. Not looking where I was going. I tripped and smacked my head a second time.

When I opened my eyes, I felt very dazed. My entire body felt stiff, I could barely move. Using all my strength I tried to sit up, but was pushed down. Confused, I looked around and to my horror I was surrounded. By not one but three maidens. Each of them was made from marble and had a large shroud covering their heads.

"Get off me!" I screamed as tears ran down my face.

My pleads were ignored as these things continued to violate my personal space. Then one raised a dagger above my chest. As soon as the blade touched my chest, I could feel the blade slice open my flesh. The pain caused me to scream and sit up like a zombie.

"Lilly" Poppy shouted. "She's awake!"

"Thank heavens?" Lilly said. "You've been out cold since Halloween. We found you passed out in the woods. What happened?"

"THE MAIDEN IN MARBLE!" I screamed. "SHE WAS CHASING ME. SHE WAS GOING....."

Poppy grabbed my hand, then gave Lilly and Heather a concerned look. She leaned in.

"Nobody was chasing you?" Poppy said.

"NO SHE WALKS!" I screamed. "SHE'S REAL!"

"Are you sure you didn't have a nightmare?" Poppy continued. "Or are you faking it? So you don't have to buy the rounds for next month?"

I wasn't faking it. I could swear I had been chased. I could swear I had been surrounded, and I know what gave me this scar on my chest. You can call bullshit but I will never forget what happened to me on that Halloween night.

The Masters Man.

By

Dave Bromley.

Silas Fangburger knew he was dying, and he didn't need an expensive doctor to confirm the fact. The increasing pain from the tumour inside him, grew steadily larger heralded the inevitable outcome. Looking back, he considered life had been good to him, which was thanks to the Master. Having such a powerful guide and mentor had certainly changed his life but he couldn't help but feel it was a pity that the granting of immortality was beyond even the Master's power.

On this dark, chilly night, Fangburger sat alone at his desk in the isolated manor house. Reaching into a draw, he took out the Ouija board and laid it open in front of him. Placing the index finger of his left hand on the board, he looked downwards towards the floor and intoned;

"Master, guide my finger, show me to whom I must pass the honour."

His finger started moving slowly from one letter to the next. Fangburger noted down each letter on a sheet of paper. After the eighth, the finger movement stopped. What he had written made little sense, which was unusual. The Master's messages were normally crystal clear.

R-T-I-M-I-N-U-S

What could this mean? Silas struggled to make sense of the message. It was not an anagram, acronym, synonym or any code that he could decipher. Only when, as a last desperate measure, he switched on the computer and visited the social media sites did he find his answer. It was like a baffling crossword clue, so simple once you knew the solution.

Relieved, Silas allowed his thoughts to drift back to the day the Master first called to him. At the time he had no job, no food or prospects, but this low point there had been the visitation. That was over twenty years ago, just after he had lost his job as an encyclopaedia salesman. He had gone to bed as usual but lay tossing and turning, worrying about his future. It was then the miracle occurred; the Master appeared to him as an ethereal, floating head and hanging over him and spoke,

"Silas Fangburger, I have chosen you to be my man on Earth."

Silas's heart raced, and his pulse pounded as he gulped in air as quietly as possible.

"Why me?"

"Because you are a slimy toad who will serve me well."

Silas was by now shaking in terror. "Go away, leave me alone." he screeched at the head.

"Believe me. Tomorrow I will give you a sign and you will follow it, and buy a Ouija board."

"I don't have money for food, and even if I did, I would not waste it on a game."

"You will have, believe me and I assure you this is no game." Then the vision slowly evaporated back into the ether.

Silas lay awake for the rest of the night trying to make sense of it and by the morning he had persuaded himself that eating those radishes before going to bed had been a mistake, but it had been all there was in his fridge.

By nature, Silas was not a gambler, however, next day the proof the Master promised materialised. Outside his local newsagents was a sign advertising the National Lottery. Searching through his pockets, he discovered he had just enough money for one ticket. On a mad impulse, over which he seemed to have no control, he entered the shop and bought a ticket for that night's draw. Once again outside the shop, he realised how foolish he had been. Now, he was penniless, but looking down into the gutter he saw a twenty-pound note. Some might call it chance or luck, but pocketing the note, Silas saw it as a sign from the Master.

That evening he watched the draw on television and became more and more excited as one by one his numbers came out of the machine. It was the largest win since the start of the National Lottery and suddenly he had turned from pauper to multi-millionaire. This was all the proof Silas needed to know the visitation was more than the result of eating a stale radish. From that point, Silas became the Devil's Man on Earth. Next morning, he contacted Camelot to claim his prize, and then went out and purchased a Ouija board.

From that day on, not only had he gone from poverty to wealth but gained the Midas touch; investing most of his winnings. His wealth continued to multiply under the Master's guidance, and although he funded rebel armies, corrupt regimes and nasty people around the world, his personal wealth continued to grow. He sponsored several wars, hundreds of protest movements, and some believed at least one successful United States Presidential candidate.

***

Back in the present he was still sat at his desk the following morning, Silas called a local solicitor and wrote a brief letter. Twenty-four hours later he was dead and, on his way down to join the Master.

***

Russell Timinus was a pleasant young man. He would help old ladies across the road and never passed a flag or Big Issue seller without donating. At twenty-four, his life had settled down into a fairly regular pattern. He worked in the local library as assistant librarian and lived in a small one-bedroom flat above a flower shop.

He was not a passionate man. His few forays with the opposite sex had proved uneventful and his primary interests remained, playing cricket for a local club and cycling. No doubt had the letter from Sprogget, Sprogget and Sprogget, solicitors and commissioners of oaths not dropped through his letter box life would have followed a steady progression and in time he would have married a Cynthia or Debora and produced a brood of equally average children. But the letter did arrive, addressed to R. Timinus.

Opening the letter, Russell skimmed through the contents in disbelief and then looked again at the envelope. Yes, it definitely it was his name and address. The heading of the brief letter read:

Re. The Estate of the late Silas Fangburger,

Mr R Timinus

Could you please contact this office as soon as possible? We have information of some importance to you.

Signed S.Sprogget.

What that information could be, he could not guess, having never heard of a Silas Fangburger. There must have been some mistake, but he decided he would call the solicitors to sort it out the following day

The next morning, he phoned Sprogget, Sprogget and Sprogget and agreed to visit their office during his lunch hour. Russell had never been to a solicitor's office before and was not quite sure what to expect, but it turned out to be a very modern and busy establishment. Once he had given his name, the pretty receptionist showed him into the office of someone she called 'young' Mr Sprogget.

The Mr Sprogget sitting behind his desk looked far from young, being nearer seventy than sixty. Rising and offering his hand, 'young' Mr Sprogget exuded an air of assured confidence.

"Good afternoon, Mr. Timinus, so good of you to come in to see us. I'm Simon Sprogget, please to meet you," he said,

"Please to meet you?" said Russell.

"Now I assume you have come about Mr Fangburger's will."

"Yes, you see I received this letter, but I'm sure there has been some sort of mistake. I have never, met or even heard of Mr Fangburger."

"No, I assure you there has been no mistake. We had a little difficulty tracking you down, but you are definitely the person we sought."

"Really?"

"Yes, really," said Sprogget, opening a folder he had on his desk. "You are Russell George Timinus, born in this very town in 1997, you went to St Peter's Comprehensive, and then Hull University."

"Yes."

"Your interests are playing cricket and cycling. Is that correct? "

"Yes, I'm secretary for the Albury Cricket Club and a member of the Road Rider's Cycle Club,"

"Yes, and you have recently taken part in a hundred-mile charity cycle ride in aid of a cancer charity."

"Yes, I did, but how did..."

"How did I know, as I said, our search for you has been most thorough and I can assure you there has been no mistake. You are the person mentioned in Mr Fangburger's will. I wrote it myself with his butler and house-keeper as witnesses. That was only hours before the poor man passed away. So, I assure that there is no mistake."

"Did you say poor man?"

"I was talking figuratively. Mr Fangburger was far from poor and he has left everything to you."

"Everything?"

"That's correct. His house at Devils Court, a cottage in the grounds, about a hundred acres of land and his fortune. His considerable fortune."

"How considerable?"

"We are not totally certain at the moment, most of it being tied up in investments, which we are still unravelling. Mr Fangburger was a very successful but secretive man. I would think at least a hundred or possibly two hundred. "

"Pounds?" said Russell.

"No, Mr Timinus, millions."

"Do you mind if I sit down for a moment?"

"No, of course not. I'm sure this news must come as a shock."

Mr Sprogget went on to talk about such things as tax and probate, but Russell was not listening. His only thought was of the magnificent sky-blue racing cycle in the window of Pedal Power, the local cycle shop. How he had wanted to buy it, but it was well out of his price range, but now… perhaps? His reverie was broken when the solicitor said,

"But I should warn you, there is a condition attached."

"Condition, what condition?"

"You must take up residence at Devil's Court. I must admit on my one visit, I found it a somewhat dismal building . Very dark and dingy. I might also say a little menacing, but I am sure you could brighten it up with a lick of paint and some imagination," said the solicitor, " the will stipulates you must sleep in the house for a year and a day."

"From when?" asked Russell.

"The first of the month following being told of the inheritance, which of course is today. In twenty days', time,

"And if I don't?"

"You lose everything."

"I still don't understand. Why me?" said Russell.

"How can I put it? I only met Mr Fangburger once, the day before he died. He had called me to his house to draw up his will. There was a strange married couple looking after him as butler and housekeeper. The Blakes who acted as witnesses to the will."

"But that doesn't explain why?" insisted Russell.

"Let me put it this way, Mr Fangburger was what you might call deluded. He told me he was the servant of someone he called the Master, and that you had been appointed to replace him."

" Appointed by who? And when you say deluded, do you mean he was a complete nutter?"

"I couldn't possibly comment on that you will have to draw your own conclusions. But he was sane enough to make his will. All I need to do now is to get you to sign a couple of documents, and I can give you the keys and directions for Devil's Court. The Blakes live in a cottage on the grounds and we have kept them on to look after the place until you decide what you want to do."

***

The papers signed and with directions on how to find Devil's Court and a cheque for £25,000, which Mr Sprogget had given him as he said, 'to tide him over, until probate is granted'. Russell left the solicitor's office meaning to go back to the library, but strangely found himself standing in front of the Pedal Power shop window. Taking the solicitor's cheque from his pocket, he studied it before walking into the shop. A few minutes later, he emerged carrying the sky-blue racing cycle.

***

The next weekend, Russell decided to miss a fifty-mile cycle ride with the Road Riders and the opportunity to show off his new bicycle. Instead he cycled out to Devil's Court. At first, despite the solicitor's directions, he had difficulty in finding the house which was not signposted, and lay well back off the road at the end of a long winding drive.

It was a chilly day, and black clouds hung heavily over the sky, threatening rain at any moment. Feeling more like an interloper than the new owner, Russell dismounted and pushed his bike up the drive. He had gone a quarter of a mile before the house came into view. It was a dark, sombre building in the gothic style, with a three-story tower on the right side of the house and a large oak front door at the base. The rest of the house was two stories high, with casement leaded glass windows and barge boards running below the tiled roof. He could also see smoke rising from two of the four chimneys.

He started towards the front door of the forbidding house but then stopped. Something seemed to be holding him back and after standing for a couple of minutes, Russell turned and pushed his bicycle back down the drive.

In the following weeks he made several visits to Sprogget, Sprogget and Sprogget and on the last day of the month was told that probate had been officially granted and he was now the official owner of Devil'/s Court and the Fangburger millions.

As the flat above the flower shop came fully furnished, he packed his few worldly goods in two suitcases and forwarded them to Devil's Court with 'Stan, a man with a van.'

On the morning of the first he once more cycled the ten miles to Devil's Court. This time peddling up the drive. but on reaching the house diffidently leant his bike up against the wall by the front door. Taking the large metal devil shaped knocker, he tapped gently on the door. After several minutes, a man in his forties dressed as though he had just walked off the set of Downton Abbey or Upstairs and Downstairs opened the door. It was Blake, every inch the popular idea of a butler.

"Yes?"

"I'm Russell Timinus, I believe Mr Sprogget told you I would be coming."

"Yes, he did, Sir. I am Blake.

It was obvious from his expression that whatever image the butler had of the new owner of Devil's Court; it was not the lycra clad, helmet holding, twenty-four-year-old who stood in front of him.

"Come in, Sir, and let me be the first to welcome you to Devil's Court. Your luggage has arrived and I have unpacked it and placed the items in your bedroom."

When he stepped into the hall of the dismal house, Russell had an overwhelming desire to turn and run; it was only the thought of the Fangburger millions and the good he could do with the money which stopped him fleeing. There would be so much he could do for the poor and starving and he determined to meet the conditions of the will come Hell or high water. Little did he realise the part Hell was going to play.

During the next hour, Blake took the new owner on a tour of the house, all seventeen rooms, and introduced him to Mrs Blake, the housekeeper. At the end of the tour, Russell asked the butler,

"Who looks after the garden, it looked very impressive when I came up the drive?"

"That's old Tom. He comes up from the village. Mrs Blake and I have very little to do with him, a common type you might say. Mr Sprogget indicated you would keep the staff on, for the time being at least."

"Oh, yes, definitely," said Russell.

"Then if you will excuse me, Sir, I will get about my duties."

"Of course," said Russell.

Left to his own devices, Russell went for a walk in the garden. Outside at the back of the house, he could see an ancient man digging in the vegetable patch.

"Hallo, you must be Tom. I'm Russell, I've sort of inherited this place."

"Oh, yes, Sir, so I heard. You'll be a bit of a change from Mr Fangburger, I reckon."

"Maybe, but to be honest I never knew him."

"Oh, funny old bugger, he was," said the old man, "now that reminds me I have a message for you, Sir."

"A message. Who from?"

"That I couldn't say, but the message is, if a time comes, and I'm sure it will, and you need rescuing, just call on old Tom. I've given you the message and if you'll excuse me, Sir, I'll have to get these spuds dug out or Mrs Blake will have my hide and that would never do." Turning his back on Russell the old man returned to his digging.

Russell couldn't think of any situation in which he would require rescue by old Tom. Shaking his head, he walked slowly back to the house. At a loss to know what to do next, he wandered aimlessly from room to room, opening drawers and cupboards just to see what was inside. In the study, he opened the desk drawer and discovered a letter addressed to R. Timinus. Opening it, he read:

Dear R.Timinus,

If you are reading this, it means I am dead and you are now the Master's Man. Guard the Ouija Board and he will contact you.

S.Fangburger

Short, sweet and total rubbish. The old fool must have been off his rocker, Russell thought, screwing up the note and throwing it into the fire.

In the afternoon, to lift his gloom, he explored the local area on his new cycle. He had a pleasant ride and on his return was in a more cheerful mood. The sky-blue machine had proved as good as he thought it would be and worth every penny. He had stayed out longer than he intended and just had time to shower and change before the gong sounded for dinner.

The meal was a solitary affair. Sitting alone at one end of a long refectory table in the large dining room, he automatically ate the three-course meal and drank the two glasses of wine, without registering any of the tastes.

Having finished the meal by eight o'clock, Russell was not sure what to do next. There did not appear to be a television or a radio in the house and had brought nothing with him to read; neither had he seen any reading material in the house. Blake then appeared to inform him unless there was anything else, he and Mrs Blake would go back to their cottage for the night.

Sitting alone and miserable at nine o'clock, Russell gave in, deciding to go upstairs to his bedroom on the third floor of the tower. It was as depressing as all the other rooms in the house and made even worse by the dark brown flocked wallpaper with hideous zombie images depicted in the design. Undressing, he got into the large four-poster bed, and after several hours, eventually fell into an uneasy sleep. He did not know how long it was before he was suddenly awoken by an earth-shattering scream followed by an absolute silence which seemed to blanket the room. The bedroom had turned icy cold, and a moaning and wailing broke the silence. As the noise, reached a crescendo the zombies detached themselves from the wallpaper, increasing in size as they did so and began circling above his pillow. Russell pulled the sheet over his head as the sound of an approaching drum beat replaced the wailing, getting louder and louder but then an eerie silence fell over the room, which was even more frightening than the drums.

Suddenly, a gigantic head appeared hovering above Russell and the zombies retreated quickly back into the wallpaper.

The head then spoke in a loud, sonorous tone.

"Raoul, Raoul, this is the Master, speak to me."

Russell lifted his head above the bedclothes, from where he had sought refuge.

"There is no Raoul here," he said in a quavering voice.

"What do you mean, are you not Raoul Timinus from San Paolo?"

"No, I'm Russell Timinus from Albury."

"Fangburger, you idiot, you have cocked it up again."

"I'm sorry, Master," said another invisible voice.

With his heart racing and covered in perspiration, Russell realised his whole body was shaking. The head slowly started to fade away, as the ceiling began slowly descending, and the side walls closing in. Russell believed his last moments had come and that both he and the fourposter would become crushed out of existence. He leapt from the bed and made for the door, but it would not open. The ceiling was now only inches above his head, and if he put both arms out, he could have touched the side walls. Just when he thought his last had come, there was a crashing sound and the door burst open. Russell felt his shoulders being grabbed and realized someone was physically hauling him out of the room.

To his amazement, once he was outside of the room. He could see his rescuer had been old Tom, but not so old now, a much younger and stronger version. He half carried and half pulled Russell out of the bedroom and down the stairs to the front door while the drum beats began again, becoming louder and louder. Tom opened the heavy front door and pushed Russell out into the cold night air.

"Run," shouted Tom, "Run for your life."

And he ran. Less than a minute later, from a hundred and fifty yards away, Russell heard a tremendous explosion as a thunderbolt crashed through the roof of Devil's Court. Turning, Russell could see that all that remained of the house was a pile of smouldering rubble.

***

The next morning, Russell sat in. Mr Sprogget's office.

"I suppose this means I shall lose the inheritance," Russell said.

"Not at all," the solicitor replied. "Why should you?"

"I can hardly sleep in a house that no longer exists."

"That is true, but I have studied the will. What it simply states is you have to sleep at Devil's Court, which is the name of the estate. It does not say the house at Devil's Court. The Blakes and all their possessions seem to have disappeared overnight and, even more peculiar, is the fact that no one in the village has ever heard of any old Tom living there. It is all very puzzling. However, my legal opinion is that as the Blake's cottage is now empty you could move in and if you slept there for the year that would meet the conditions of the will."

"Are you sure?"

"Certain, trust me I'm a solicitor"

That day Russell moved into the cottage and after twelve months, he became adjusted to being a very wealthy man and discovered he enjoyed the benefits of being filthy rich. The good life suited him. Although he could not imagine why, Russell had become very popular with the ladies, both young and old, and found that he enjoyed their attention. Unfortunately, he became so busy enjoying himself that he never quite got around to making the donations to the poor and starving he had originally intended.

During the year he spent in the cottage, Russell had what remained of the old house removed and a new home built to his specifications. The new Devil's Court suited him very well and he threw many fantastic parties for all his newfound friends. Occasionally, Russell would seek solitude and take out the Ouija board, but none of his friends knew why he did this. In the triple garage alongside his shining new Daimler lay a sky-blue cycle forgotten, neglected and covered in dust.

The Disappearance of Janet Mayfair.

By

Gemma Owen-Kendall.

No one knew what happened to Janet Mayfair, some say she was murdered, some say she killed herself and others say she was abducted by aliens. My task as a ghost hunter was to try and connect with Janet and get those all important answers of her disappearance. I needed to know for sure what happened to her. From interviews with family and friends, my understanding was that Janet Mayfair was a middle aged lady who lived on her own at the cottage of Buttercup Fields. She didn't have any pets but she always had a hanging basket of nuts out for the birds. Her cottage was slightly run down on the outside décor, a poison ivy plant had outgrown itself and covered up most of the front. The cottage stood on its own slightly above the village of Toad Suck. It was often witnessed having a faint light on since Janet's disappearance.

Tonight, I was staying inside the cottage of Buttercup Fields, every ghost hunt mission I do, I'm always escorted by Fred and out cameraman Ryan. The three of us have investigated many buildings to be haunted by ghosts.

There was something about my recent case to study that made me uneasy. I had that gut feeling that we were about to embark on something so evil and sinister. It was half past ten at night by the time we reached Buttercup Fields cottage, as I opened the front door the smell of gone off eggs pungent through the air. The smell was too unbearable for me but I always came equipped with a gas mask for incidents like this. The cottage hadn't been occupied for some time, for many months now. The temperature in the air felt icy cold and I could sense a chill down my spine.

As we set up our equipment in the living room, a hissing sound was heard, quite like a snake. There was no electric in the cottage so we used our torches to try see if we could locate where that sound was coming from. Gradually the hissing sound stopped and there was silence for a while. Ryan now has his camera at the ready se we could properly start our investigation. We headed to the master bedroom where a dusty and mouldy bed stood. As I shined the torch around, I came across a crumpled envelop on the worn out bedside table. It was not addressed to anybody. I picked it up and showed it to Fred then towards the camera.

"I'm going to open this; it could be a clue with what happened to Janet." I carefully tore open the envelop without trying to rip any of it as it felt so delicate. As I read out what what written in smudgy ink, the icy cold temperature suddenly changes to really hot. The heat was too much that I had to leave the master bedroom. Fred and

Ryan followed very close behind me, how in the hell did that happen? We quickly rushed back to the living room where all our equipment was. The temperature had gone back to that icy cold feeling. I slumped onto one of the dusty chairs as I looked back upon the words handwritten on the letter. Everything that had happened to us so far was stated in this letter. Would we make it out of here alive?

No Clip.

By

Ants Ambridge.

Grifffromdamarsh: So how the fuck does that make me an SJW cuck?

Def2noobs: Keep crying PC baby

Weeb4lyf: rollingeyes.emoji

Grifffromdamarsh: Spawn camping is what losers do, all I'm saying.

Def2noobs: 1v1 me then, fag.

Grifffromdamarsh: Sure. No spawn camping or GTFO

Weeb4lyf: donkeyface.emoji   donkeyface.emoji pepethefroggrin.emoji

Brian sighed. He'd been plugging away on Twitch for two months now, trying to establish himself on the platform. His audience was slowly growing, but not at the rate he'd like. Not at the rate needed for the illustrious Twitch partnership programme; the next step in making his hobby a potential career. Brian watched the chat monitor scrolling through as Griff and Def bickered. They were his most regular viewers, and also his most toxic. They berated him daily, criticising his abilities, posting insults (disguised as 'banter') and, worst of all, back-seating. Once he'd his own mods, those two in particular were heading for the ban-hammer.

A garish pink neon outlined a cartoon cat on the screen. The cat wore shades, the shorthand for cool, and pointed at a glowing purple sign behind it; 'Kat-Chan will be airing soon!'. The cartoon cat also sported a duster coat. Brian looked at the image, his placeholder before starting his streams, and wondered if he should ask the artist to add a fedora.

Grifffromdamarsh: Where the fuck is Kat, anyway? Fucking amateur streamers man. So unprofessional.

Def2noobs: Yeah, you're a busy guy. You've got Cheetos to eat, Mountain Dew to drink and masturbatin' to do. YeeHaw. 'Murrca

Grifffromdamarsh: At least I have all my teeth, Brit fag.

Weeb4lyf: isaaccrying.emoji stfu.emoji.

Brian screwed his eyes and drew in a breath. On his main monitor, he readied the game and the software he would use for tonight's stream. He would try something a little different; to explore the out-of-bounds content of a horror game he'd previously played; Mirabelle. Mirabelle was an atmospheric first-person puzzler set in a mansion controlled by a demonic porcelain doll. As ideas went, it was certainly derivative, but something about the game had chilled Brian to his core, much to the delight of his viewers, relishing in his every squirm, erupting into laughter and a sea of emojis at his screams at the jump-scares. It was also, to date, his highest viewed stream, with edited highlights performing well on YouTube as well.

Steeling himself, Brian clicked on the icon to start his stream. His image appeared in the bottom-left corner of the screen. Brian smiled as warm and welcoming as he could fake towards the regulars already in the chat.

- Hey guys! Thanks for waiting! Got something special in mind for tonight's stream!

Def2noobs: About fucking time.

Grifffromdamarsh: I should punish you for your re-tardiness.

Weeb4lyf: prayinghands.emoji

Brian booted up the Mirabelle game from his launcher. He tried to engage with the chat as best he could without losing his temper at the entitled pricks he depended on to kick-start the rest of his audience engagement. An active chat, no matter how hostile, was encouraging to other interested parties. Streaming was not just about the content, but also the community. The view count number rose from three to seven as the Mirabelle logo filled the screen, accompanied by the sounds of thunder and icy screams.

Grifffromdamarsh: No, fuck that dude. You've already done this game. This is just lazy. It doesn't change. Play something else.

Def2noobs: For once, I agree with the dickhead. Fuck walking simulators. They are boring as shit.

Weeb4lyf: kappa.emoji kappa.emoji ?

- No Weeb, I'm not trolling. Relax guys. It isn't a straight play through, I've got some no-clip software, and I was going to run a boundary break of the game.

Def2noobs: I'll allow it. For now.

Grifffromdamarsh: OK. At least we get to laugh at your girlie squeals.

Weeb4lyf: shrug.emoji

Brian resisted the urge to glower. If these guys hated him so much, why did they show up every night? He wished they would give him something, anything, that indicated they liked him in some way. Weeb seemed OK, but only ever communicated in emojis, almost a new language he'd had to adapt to. Brian clicked the 'start game' button on screen, the motionless titular dolls porcelain lips twisting into a malevolent grin and the screen zooms into the eye, fizzling into white noise and the opening cinematic began. Whilst this played, Brian activated the no clip software, minimizing the box and placing it on the lower-right corner of the screen. The viewer count grew from seven to twelve. Strangely, only the three regulars were active in the chat.

Weeb4lyf: spookyskeleton.emoji

Grifffromdamarsh: How2hack for boomers :D

Def2noobs: Where's the dubstep? Bwwwwwaaaaaaarrrrrggghhh

Brian ignored the jibes and progressed through the introduction of the game, waiting for the entry to the mansion for the boundary breaking software fun to begin. The first-person perspective on the screen flickered as the character's arms strained to push open the heavy wooden doors with an ominous creak. The camera perspective changed to a second-person viewpoint as eyes watched the protagonist walk with trepidation into the huge, open hallway. As the camera shifted once more, it became clear, through the aid of lightning effects that the second viewpoint was that of the titular doll; motionless in a glass display cabinet. Windows glowing with moonlight reflected on the china cheeks of Mirabelle. The doll's clothes were ragged and aged, a mixture of whites, sepia browns and fag-ash yellow. Patches of hair were missing from the doll's scalp, perhaps lost to the passage of time. The character leans in for a closer inspection when a lightning flashes, creating the illusion that the lifeless eyes flick directly to the player. Despite himself, Brian flinched at the jump-scare, cursing as he did so.

- Fucks sake! I knew it was coming too!

127

Grifffromdamarsh: Hahahahahahahahahahha!

Def2noobs: Gotta admit, as boring as this game is, it nailed those lighting effects.

Weeb4lyf: pants.emoji poop.emoji

- Ok guys! Let's take a look through the walls, see what's there!

Brian's forced comradery caused derision from his regular viewers. The view count grew further, now showing thirty-five watching. On screen, the first-person perspective headed straight towards a wall adorned with a faded green wallpaper with cracked and peeling Fleur-de-Lys symbols in a diagonal pattern. The symbols filled the screen, betraying their jpeg origins, before it filled the screen with black, the reverse images of walls and doors to the character's right-hand side. Brian moved the character forwards, towards the location of the first of the game's scares, one that sees the titular doll running across the player's pathway accompanied by the giggle of a child.

Since the character was out of bounds, the audio cues had no point of reference, so once the background music reached the end, it could no longer loop. The silence echoed as Brian pitched forward into darkness, a small room emerging from the gloom and slowly filling the screen.

Grifffromdamarsh: This is dull. I'm starting a petition to change the game.

Weeb4lyf: hush.emoji

A wood panelled wall filled the screen, before Brian pushed through into the room. He flicked the camera around to check the surroundings; nothing out of the ordinary. He focussed the camera on the image of Mirabelle, the character model in the standard pose; upright with arms stretched outwards to the side, a bastardised version of a crucifixion. Brian opened his mouth to speak with his viewers, but a glitch caused the child's laughter to cue, causing a yelp of fright.

- So gu—yaaarrgggh!

Weeb4lyf: lmfao.emoji

Def2noobs: Oooohhh! The jump-scares are in slightly different places. Change the game please.

Grifffromdamarsh: I don't think Kat will, the view count has just reached 104. Your best stream ever?

- I… I… hadn't noticed. But, yeah Griff, you're right. Hey to all the new viewers!

Brian scolded himself for being so jumpy. But it made for entertaining viewing at least. He used the controller to zoom in to the doll, trying to pan around to get a close-up of the face. Frustratingly, the camera wouldn't obey his commands, hitting an invisible wall as the sides of the head became visible. This confused Brian, there should be no walls at all with no clip software. He tried to back out of the room to enter from another angle. Strange. The character appeared to be now trapped inside the small room. Brian placed his controller down as his hands operated the mouse and keyboard, re-running the software and searching for a reason it had stopped working online.

Grifffromdamarsh: Yaaaaawwwwwwwwwnnnn!

Def2noobs: Again, we agree. This guy ain't getting his hacking badge from the scouts.

Weeb4lyf: look.emoji

    With Brian distracted and frustrated, skim reading search results for a solution, the outstretched arms of Mirabelle moved. At first, almost infinitesimally, but picking up speed to a crawl. The arms lowered as the doll glided forward, the blank expression becoming a grimace as a flat, deep voice filled Brian's headphones.

-    **You're not supposed to be in here**.

    Brian didn't scream, beads of cold perspiration formed on his head. His eyes widened, glassing with tears of terror. The voice vibrated though his skull and felt as if he'd swallowed the words, causing his guts to churn. He wanted to wrench the headphones from himself and throw them against the wall and exit the game, but it froze him to his seat, seemingly mesmerised by what unfurled on the screen before him. The doll's mouth twisted into a grin. This elicited a physical response from Brian as he jumped, jerking his gaming chair to the left by two feet. The doll's eyes on screen followed his movement. Curiosity, though, tinged with fear, caused him to move side to side. Still the doll's eyes matched his movement. Brian shivered. Sod the stream, he was turning it off. He noticed the view count; 234. His best stream ever and he was disconnecting. His hand crept towards the escape key. The doll's brow furrowed.

Mirabelle1: I wouldn't do that if I were you.

Mirabelle2: I wouldn't do that if I were you.

Mirabelle3: I wouldn't do that if I were you.

Mirabelle4: I wouldn't do that if I were you.

Grifffromdamarsh: What the fuck is going on?

Mirabelle5: I wouldn't do that if I were you.

Mirabelle6: I wouldn't do that if I were you.

Weeb4lyf: shrug.emoji spooked.emoji

Mirabelle7: I wouldn't do that if I were you.

Mirabelle8: I wouldn't do that if I were you.

Def2noobs: This is a cool effect Kat, how did you do it?

The chat screen flared into life, dominated by variants of the Mirabelle bot flooding his screen with his regulars, questioning what he'd done. He closed his eyes, finger hovering over the escape key, his breathing jagged and shallow. Why was he so scared? What was the worst that could happen? The chat screen continued.

Mirabelle232: I wouldn't do that if I were you.

Mirabelle233: I wouldn't do that if I were you.

Brian gritted his teeth and stabbed at the escape key. The image on the screen began to fizzle and pop.

Mirabelle234: I warned you.

Static filled the screen, flickering between the black and white fuzz and the leering face of the video game doll. A piercing squeak of what sounded like a rusty swing filled the headphones of Brian and his viewers alike. A disorienting flickering grew rapid, becoming a strobe like effect. The webcam image of Brian, mouth widening in horror, tears spilling from his eyes, cowering in a strobe-induced twelve frames per second. The screen went blank suddenly, as the programme closed-down, Brian's image disappeared from view, replaced by only darkness.

Grifffromdamarsh: OK. I admit. That was pretty cool.

Def2noobs: And original. Well done Kat!

Weeb4lyf: applause.emoji

Brian's wallpaper backdrop appeared on screen, a white background with anime waifus in a variety of suggestive poses. The glow from the screen illuminated his image in the screen's corner. His head was bowed, a trickle of drool hanging from his mouth. Brian started to cackle, his head raising slowly as he stared into the camera. His eyes widened and his mouth widened into a wet, menacing smile. He inched towards the camera.

- Stay tuned folks! You're next!

Brian pulled his hand back and swiped at the camera, disconnecting his image from the feed. The placeholder returned. The viewer counter showed 3.

Grifffromdamarsh: Short, but definitely sweet.

Def2noobs: Yeah, it's great when streamers get creative. I'm sharing this as we speak.

Weeb4lyf: Yes, we should all do that. Share it now.

The Night Shift.

By

P.J. Brett

R ight, who's up for shots." shouts Emma getting up from her chair and knocking a glass of red wine over her friend Jennie's new dress.

"Oops sorry." Said Emma stumbling towards the bar.

A man was watching her from the other end of the bar. He was very good looking; tall and athletically built, with gorgeous brown almost black eyes. His mouth was wide and sensual, but the thing that was the most striking about the man was his thick black wavy hair which hung down long and unruly to just above his shoulders and it moved in such a way that made it look like it had a life of its own. The man had been watching her all afternoon. At first she felt flattered but now she found it creepy.

"Oh God Emma's on a bender again isn't she? Said Kristy.

"Yes, just look at my dress." Jennie replied, dabbing at the red wine stains on her dress. "She can't half knock them back. I'm surprised she can still walk."

"I hope she hasn't brought her car, the last time we went out she drove home pissed." Said Kristy. "It's a wonder she hasn't had an accident and killed someone."

"She's been very lucky up to now, but if she carries on like this she will." Replied Lucy. "You'd think a nurse would know better. I certainly wouldn't want her looking after me or one of my family members would you"?

"No I would not" said Jennie firmly.

"Shush" said Kristy "she coming back."

"Come on girls" shouted Emma raucously "let's get these shots down us."

"Whoa, slow down Emma. Have you forgotten you're at work tonight"?

"Oh Kristy it's your birthday don't be such a party pooper.

"Anyway I don't want to talk about boring work. See that man sitting at the bar? He's been looking at me all afternoon and it's creeping me out."

"What man?" said Jennie scoffed dabbing at the red wine stains on her dress. "There's no one there."

"The one at the bar with the dark hair." Said Emma.

135

"There are no men in here it's just us." Replied Jennie laughing.

Emma looked over at the bar. The man had gone.

"Right, it's time for me to go." Kristy said. "I've got to walk the kid's home from school in an hour. Thank you all for a lovely birthday afternoon."

"Oh, come on girls don't be so boring, the parties only just getting started" slurred Emma.

"Someone has to behave responsibly Emma." Kristy said sharply.

"Oh, okay." Emma said, feeling embarrassed by Kristy's response.

"Would you like me to phone you a taxi?" Said Kristy pointedly.

"No it's okay. I'll grab a coffee first then get a taxi home."

"Well make sure you do." Warned Kristy.

Emma waited until her friends had left. Her car was parked two blocks away. She had purposely parked there so her friends would not see she was driving. Luckily she managed to drive home in one piece, climbed into her bed and fell asleep.

Emma is asleep to be precise in REM sleep, this is the phase in which we dream. Emma's eyes dart backwards and forwards in quick rapid movements behind her closed eye lids, her mouth moves as if she is talking to someone, and her arms and legs thrash around like a freshly caught fish who is watching helplessly as a knife approaches nearer and nearer ready to cut off its head. She is sweating and her heartbeat and breathing are exacerbated.

In her nightmare world Emma is lost; her sight is obscured by the thick damp fog which surrounds her. She walks around aimlessly and blindly she trips over something and falls to the ground. She lays there for a few moments feeling disorientated. After a few minutes she shakily stands up, the wet mud is cold between her toes. She feels around for something to steady her and is rewarded when she touches a flat ledge just above her. Slowly and painfully she climbs up onto the cold smooth object. She shivers uncontrollably and instinctively rubs the goose flesh on her arms, teeth chattering she wraps her arms tightly around herself trying to retain any smidgen of warmth. Alone and frightened she place's her head in her hands and begins to weep. Eventually the fog begins to dissipate but not enough to stop a fine mist from clinging to her skin and hair. She realises she is in a cemetery and the hard cold object she is sitting on is in reality someone's grave. From her elevated height she scans the landscape around her, it is dusk but even in the impending darkness she soon realises that this place is devoid of any colour like a sepia toned photograph it is grey and depressing. The tall trees are menacing and gnarled forming twisted shadowy faces on their trunks, their arm like branches are sharp, distorted and elongated. Their

Arachnid clawed fingers reach out to grasp at her viciously across the dark troubled sky. She turns her head sharply glimpsing a movement in her peripheral vision, then blamed the shadows cast by the trees and dismisses it. But wait there it is again. Her eyes are drawn to a pair of marble angels stood like sentinels either side of a child's grave, sombrely guarding their charge in her eternal rest. They look at Emma in judgement and superiority, their cold eyes bore deeply into her soul, their proud wings unfurled ready to take flight. Emma shakes her head in shock and disbelief as the angels slowly descend from their plinths in unison, their movements fluid and graceful, their bodies and wings mirroring each other in perfect harmony, like a beautiful dance macabre. Their presence was hypnotic and she found herself completely in their thrall. Their angelic voices created a beautiful and captivating operatic aria and the performance pulled her towards them as a siren would a sailor. Emma was transfixed, caught like a fly in a spider's web as they gravitated slowly towards her, but she cared not. For the first time since she had found herself in this awful place she felt safe. Emma smiled at the angels but as the angels smiled back at her, Emma's smile slowly disappeared. The angel's smiles changed from one of serenity and kindness to mocking and cruelty their sardonic grins revealing large sharp fangs, quick forked tongues darted in and out of their mouths in lizard like movements. The diadems that encircled the angel's heads, gradually metamorphosed into a snake, the snakes head then divided into two, and continued its mitosis until the angels transformed into Gorgons, their heads a sea of slithering

138

snakes that moved in slow and sensual waves. Emma closed her eyes tightly, too terrified to look at them. Emma heard the hiss of the approaching snakes and curled herself tightly into ball, the pain was agonising as the Gorgons sharp talons pierced her flesh like a ripe peach, her blood felt sticky and warm on her cold skin. She momentarily rose into the air then plummeted downwards, moving faster and faster like Alice falling down the White Rabbits burrow.

After what seemed an age, the Gorgons threw Emma to the ground like a bundle of rags she looked around her, the terrain was bleak and unwelcoming a large bank of fog enveloped them, pressing down upon them like a dead weight. The sky was leaden and dull as if an impending storm were imminent. The temperature dropped further with each step they took across the vast landscape. They carried on until there were no paths left to follow the terrain consisted of rocks and nothing else. The light was rapidly diminishing to a sky now heavy and black.

Eventually they saw some people. Their heads cast downwards cradled in their hands, as if in the pits of despair they appeared almost lifeless. Gloom and desolation radiated from them in dark depressing waves. So enveloped where these pitiful souls in their despondency they never even noticed them pass by. Their homes were little more than hovels and were disturbing to look at, and a lingering fetid odour filled the air that reminded he of rotting flesh like rotting flesh. Emma knew instinctively that the conditions these people lived in were the rewards they had earned for themselves when they had lived upon the earth. The further they journeyed the worse the conditions became. Here in these dark lands all was bleak and forbidding the lighting was so dark you could barely see. Occasionally Emma would catch a glimpse of some of the inhabitants as they passed along. Some were unmistakably evil showing the life of vice they had led upon the earth. Their bodies malformed and distorted mirrored their evil minds. They passed whole bands of seemingly demented souls unmistakably on their way to some potential evil intent.

A cacophony of mad raucous laughter mixed with screams filled the air The Darkness surrounded them like a cloak, heavy and foul. The road they followed was precipitous and jagged. Emma exhausted and on the point of collapse slipped down one of the many fissures in the rocks which were covered in a repugnant dirty green slime, but no mercy was shown by the Gorgons who hauled to her feet and pushed her onwards. They journeyed downwards for what seemed an age, finding them half way down an immense crater many miles in circumference. The sides of the crater dangerous and menacing loomed above them. The whole area below them was scattered with huge masses of rock, as though some enormous cataclysmic event had disrupted them from the rim of the crater and sent them crashing down into the depths below forming natural caves and tunnels.

A noxious vapour rose from the caves and tunnels below them and rising with the vapour was an abhorrent feeling of intense hatred and looming harm. Looking through the miasma they could see all kinds of hideous creatures crawling over the upper surfaces of the rocks below and although you wouldn't believe it they had once been human beings. They reached a natural shelf and finally came to a halt roughly fifteen feet from the bottom of the huge crater overlooking the chaos below. The Gorgons pushed her closer and closer to the edge.

"No please don't." She begged. "Show some mercy."

But her cries fell on deaf ears. She felt a shove as the Gorgons pushed her from the ledge. She hit the ground with a large thud and everything went black.

Emma woke up choking and vomited as acrid liquid hit the back of her throat. Three hideous creatures surrounded her. The largest of the three creatures laughed as it urinated on her as if marking his territory, encouraged by two slightly smaller but no less revolting creatures. Evil radiated from their every pore. A scream erupted from deep within her, the sound raw and guttural like a terrified, wounded animal. She scuttled back on all fours in panic. She could feel the wet sloppy mud between her fingers and it took a second to realise that it was not mud that she was laid in, but a sea of foul bodily fluids. These creatures had lived filthy obscene lives on the earth and were now paying for their actions in the conditions they had made for themselves. She didn't want to look around her but she couldn't help it, and the horrors that were going on around her made her believe that she was insane. Everywhere around her laughing, snarling packs of beasts were consumed in unspeakable acts of debauchery and violence. The noise was incessant and relentless. Without warning one of the three beasts grabbed her by the hair, the pain in her scalp burned like fire, as bloody clumps of her hair was ripped out by its sharp talons. Another of the three punched her in the face and laughed in glee as her nose burst with a loud crunch. The creature laughed as it pulled her to him; its large, slimy, slug like tongue slithered out of its mouth and licked her bloody nose with delight. Its face contorted grotesquely in ecstasy as it savoured the taste of her blood. The dominant and most powerful of the group stepped forward grabbed Emma and threw her to the floor it stood in front of her and began to unbutton what remained of its tattered breeches. The other creatures grabbed excitedly at her clothing, ripping her skin in their frenzy. When the last of her clothing had been ripped from her body and she was left naked and vulnerable the dominant creature pinned Emma down forcing her legs open. The other two fought over who would be next. Emma paralysed with fear closed her eyes and prayed to God for mercy, and in the twinkling of an eye she found herself back in the cemetery.

Standing in front of her is a girl of around eight years of age in her hand she is holding a red balloon; her long curls, once beautiful are nothing more than matted dirty clumps sticking out of her bloody scalp. Her face is mummified and skeletal, her eyes once blue are now empty and maggot ridden. She child opens her mouth to speak and thousands of tiny spiders hatch from it. Emma recoils in horror; she can smell the death and decay on the child's breath as she whispers

"They're coming for you".

Emma sat bolt upright in bed, her heart racing from her nightmare. God she needed a drink, reaching for the glass of water on her bedside table she noticed the clock,

"Shit, Shit I'm late", she cursed. Throwing off her quilt, she raced towards the shower and tripped over her cat Salem on the way.

"Sorry Salem" she croaked, her throat dry.

She showered, made herself a quick cup of coffee and raced to her car. She sat behind the wheel feeling sick and dizzy, she took some deep breathes and a few sips of water and drove off into the cold night. She had less than half an hour to get to work and the Journey would take at least an hour and fifteen minutes. It was an agency shift for a hospital out in the sticks. She had not worked there before and was not at all sure how to get there.

"Shit" she cursed loudly. She had forgotten to feed Salem before she left. She picked up her mobile phone rang the number and put it on speaker.

"Hello Emma I was just on my way over how are you"?

"Oh damn. Sorry Mum I forgot you were coming over! I've booked an agency shift tonight sorry"

The woman on the other end sounded disappointed.

"Oh I didn't think you were working tonight, didn't you go to Kristy's birthday brunch today"? Said Emma's mum with an accusatory tone to her voice.

"Yes mum and before you ask I only drank coffee".

"I hope so. You do remember what date it is today don't you? Are you sure you haven't had a drink you sound a bit funny"?

"Oh Mum don't go on I made a promise not to drink anymore didn't I, and of course I remember what day it is."

Emma had in fact not remembered the day her mum was referring to.

"Yes you did promise me"! Because if it were too happened again I couldn't lie for you like I did last time. It's been hell living with that awful guilt, thinking about what those parents must have gone through and are still going through. It will never be over for them, not knowing who killed their little girl".

"I've told you Mum I don't drink anymore let alone drink and drive. Now please can we just drop the subject?" Emma shouted at her mother.

There was a few seconds silence before Emma spoke.

"I'm sorry Mum I shouldn't have shouted at you like that, I'm just stressed because I'm late for work. I was just about to call you to see if you would feed Salem for me?"

"Well I'll have to go back to my house because I haven't got your spare key with me Said Emma's Mum sounding angry.

"You know I love you don't you Mum".

There was a few more seconds' silence.

"What time will you be getting up after your shift tomorrow? I want to show you something". She said placated, and sounding excited.

"I should be up by two, so shall we make it three pm."

"Yes ok I'll see you tomorrow then. Love you."

"Love you too. Bye".

It was warm in the car and Emma began to feel sleepy so she opens the window and turned the radio on. She doses off at the wheel because the next thing she hears is a car horn blaring. Slamming on her brakes she sees the other car swerve trying to avoid her, it loses control then hit a tree. Emma did not stop.

"Hi I'm Emma. Sorry I'm late but I had some car trouble on the way here".

Emma looked at the senior nurse, she was very tall and slim with flawless marble skin and beautiful long dark curls swept up into a messy bun on top of her head. Emma realised that she was staring at her and looked away embarrassed.

"Oh don't worry I'm just glad you turned up. Is your car alright now"?

"Yes its fine just needed a jump start".

"Oh well that's good then."

"Well my name's Julia and this is Paul our Porter, who's also happens to be my twin brother smiles Julia."

"Hello" said Paul.

Emma looked at Paul; he seemed familiar somehow, he was very handsome with the same flawless skin as his sister, tall with a muscular build and mop of unruly dark wavy hair.

"Have you ever worked bank shifts for other hospitals Paul? You just look familiar that's all."

"No one job is enough for me," smiled Paul.

"It's your first time with us isn't." Asked Julia.

Emma nodded in response.

"As you know from when I spoke to you on the phone this is a high observation unit. We only have three patients tonight; unfortunately they're very ill and there doesn't look much chance of them surviving so it's just a case of monitoring them closely and keeping them as pain free as possible."

"So what would you like me to do"?

"Well to be honest there isn't that much to do tonight. So I'll sit with the patients and monitor them if that's ok? If you could man the phone's and let me know if there are any new admission expected, that would be great. If you need me I will be in cubicle four."

"Okay I will keep you posted."

Emma made herself a coffee and sat at the nurses' station. A couple of hours later she heard a cough and opened her eyes. She saw Paul standing at the other side of the desk.

"Sorry Paul can I help you."

"Yes, Julia asked me to inform you that the family have passed away."

"Oh I didn't know it was a family."

"Yes it's very sad we've already taken them down to the mortuary. She asked if you could take down some mortuary cards and help with last offices please. The cards are in the second right hand drawer."

"Where's the mortuary?" asked Emma.

"It's in the basement. Don't worry I'll show you were it is."

Emma grabbed the cards from the draw and followed Paul to the mortuary. It was cold and dark. Julia had gathered everything they needed to wash and wrap up the bodies. Julia and Paul pulled back the sheets from the first two bodies. Emma stared at them in disbelief and began shaking with shock she felt dizzy and faint.

"No, sobbed Emma hysterically that's my Mum and Dad, God no, please tell me this isn't true." She cried her voice breaking with emotion.

"Yes we're afraid it's true," said Paul and Julia very matter- of- factly and in unison as if speaking as one. They stood side by side very calmly showing no emotion on their pale faces, they reminding Emma of the marble statues in her dream.

"Have you no compassion." She sobbed.

"Twelve years ago today you killed an eight year old girl. You had been drinking heavily and drove home. She ran out into the road chasing her red balloon. You didn't see her until it was too late and your reactions were slower because you were drunk. You ran over her small body and didn't stop leaving her like a broken doll in the middle of the road in excruciating pain until she died. So please do not talk to us about compassion. Hissed Paul and Julia together.

148

"But I was only eighteen I'm not that person anymore. I gave up drinking after the accident, I'm a nurse I help people." Emma protested trying to convince them she had changed.

"You're not only a murderer but you're also a liar." Continued Paul How do you feel knowing you lied to your mother before you killed her and your father?"

"What do you mean I killed them, I didn't kill them?" Emma retorted.

"Are you sure about that? Do you remember the conversation you had with your mum on the way to work this evening? She wanted to come round to your house to show you something tomorrow afternoon." She was so excited about it. She was excited because she wanted to show you her new car, the same car that you thought had swerved and avoided hitting you and ended up hitting a tree instead. Your parents died because you had been drinking and fell asleep at the wheel."

"But who's the third person?"

Paul and Julia smiled a cruel smile revealing large sharp fangs and forked tongues which darted quickly in and out of their mouths in lizard like movements, their dark curly hair began to writhe and transform into a sea of slithering snakes. The Gorgons now fully transformed lifted the third sheet revealing Emma's broken twisted body on the mortuary slab. Then Emma screamed like a terrified wounded animal as a child with a red balloon appeared beside her and whispered

"They are coming for you."

The Underworld.

By

H.O. Ward.

In dark and silent alleyways

Betwixt the neon street,

Exists an evil underworld

You never want to meet.

When sun descends and shadows fall,

Trolls they stalk the alley wall.

Dogs they scarper to survive

As the alley begins to come alive.

Cats they hiss with glowing eyes

That call to you with baby cries.

Bats through darkness swoop and flutter,

While all along the alleys gutter

Rats they scurry to and fro,

Where you never really ought to go.

Owls they hoot in eerie chorus,

And evil starts to gently call us.

Betwixt the bins and refuse sack

Where everything looks dark and black,

Witches hide their warts and face,

And ghouls wait in a shadowed place,

Until the magic witching hour,

And darkness fills with evil power.

When midnight strikes

And the moon is full,

The underworld is waiting,

With evil in the making.

Towards the neon flooded street

Darkness spills, inviting you

On breath that gently whispers.

Step inside, come to me,

My brothers and my sisters.

The Hidden Stairs.

By

Caroline Beeson Spence.

We lived together; 4 - 17 year olds, enjoying life and mucking in together. This was our first time living away from our parents. Life was exciting. Louise had a car. A beautiful, blue mini, ready to be used and abused by all of us, taking us on our adventures out in the countryside and away from the house.

Louise had the biggest bedroom, overlooking the street with two big windows, flooding the room with light. The energy in the room was positive and clear.

My room was next to this, not quite able to benefit from the light of those two huge windows and constantly drawn back towards the back of the house. It was hard to understand why I was being drawn to the back of the house.

Nick had the smallest bedroom, directly off the hall and next to Michelle's. Nick's bedroom overlooked the neighbour's garden but the energy in the hallway drew you back into the house rather than towards the view of the outside.

Michelle had the big bedroom at the back overlooking the garden and the undertaker's premises. She could see the comings and goings of the dead at all times of the day and night. The dead would be moved from hospitals and homes in a black vehicle with darkened windows. With the care and reverence the situation deserved, the undertaker slid them out of the vehicle to their temporary resting homes while they waited for their final resting place, a journey to be undertaken with loved ones.

The house was on a busy road; Manor Avenue, full of families and friends and was a thoroughfare to the town centre from an ancient part of town. Humans from Abbeys, Monasteries and Convents had all accessed the road on their daily travels.

Parties took place regularly and we all enjoyed our friendship and invited others to the house. Neighbours complained and police visited. The night-time economy profited from our meagre incomes from part time jobs in chip shops and frozen food emporiums. Our entwined lives were bright and forward-looking.

I hadn't lived there long when I had my first encounter with the hidden stairs. An early night beckoned, and a dream arrived. I wasn't sure if I was awake or actually asleep. The light was vivid, and fog filled the hallway along the corridor upstairs. Leaving my bedroom, I climbed down the small set of stairs, moving onto a different level, holding onto the bannister with white knuckles for safety. I tiptoed down the hallway to see where the fog was leading me.

154

The hall to Michelle and Nick's bedrooms had extended, I was puzzled. The light shone out of the wall between 2 bedrooms, another staircase had appeared. Whether awake or asleep I knew that this was not really there, but I could not stop myself from climbing the stairs to another level of the house which had appeared through the fog. Another bannister secured my safety on the stairs.

The icy atmosphere was slowly revealed. My breath contributed to the fog; I pulled my pyjamas closer around me. It gave no comfort. The stairs opened onto a huge space with dark wooden floorboards, The fog cloaked the full space, there were no windows, just dust and dark and old floorboards. I started to shiver and feel the extreme cold. The fear of the space permeated my very being. A noise came out of me that I could not control – wooooooooOOOOOOOOOOOOO.

The fearful noise startled me more. I had been asleep, my unintentional noise woke me. It started quietly and rose to a crescendo of fear. It was not a deliberate noise, nothing like a spoken word or shout. It was a guttural reaction to the fear of the situation. The fog disappeared, the hall closed up and the fear remained. It was 2.27am.

I began to hate going to sleep in that house. Visitations to the other level in the cold punctuated my sleep regularly. I became exhausted by my broken sleep as I tried to explore the other level. The life with my friends was being overshadowed with the noise of fear at 2.27am. I had to leave it, I couldn't sleep, my time there was done.

Life moved on and became busier. The memory of fear faded. I married, had my family and my boys kept me busy and safe from dreams due to the utter exhaustion of parenthood. As they grew, a house move took us to another home in the wildnerness of County Durham. Fear returned as my brain allowed space for other worldliness in my sleep.

High Stables was the pit that the Pit Manager's home, Pontop House served. The Farrier lived in the adjoining cottage and relics from those long gone days could be found in the stables, under the floorboards, in fields and the forest. We'd weave stories around those relics of life lived in the space before we inhabited it.

WooooooooOOOOOOOOOOOOOOOOOOOO woke me. What had I seen, what had I felt, am I still asleep? Rubbing my eyes, it came back to me. I put the light on. I knew I would not see anything but I felt the need to light the fear out of my bedroom.

I knew it was a young woman. Where had she gone? She entered my bedroom at the door, although I didn't see it open and she walked across the floor in a Victorian gown with the fabric rustling as she moved. Diagonally across my room. The door wasn't open, she just appeared, walked with purpose and disappeared. The room had become icy cold. It was 2.27am.

Nightmares visited me to bring the hidden stairs and the woman in my bedroom to life. I'd know that I was dreaming and spaces not there would be linked to real

156

spaces and they'd appear over and over. A frozen ballroom with black curtains appeared regularly. I daren't go in, I'd know the fear I would feel before I entered. Once I'd gone in, I'd pull the curtains to one side to find the light but it was always dark and icy with fog cloaking the view.

Please no more. I wrestled with my thoughts to try and force a choice into the situation. She visited me on many occasions over the years and my noise woke me each time.

Life moved on, small boys grew and years later, I moved to a house in close proximity to Manor Avenue. Daily reminders of the hidden stairs started to punctuate my day. My brain took me back to that time.

WoooooooOOOOOOOOOOOO, every night, my own voice waking me up after a visit to the frozen upper level of Manor Avenue or deep memories of the lady walking across my bedroom. The clock reflected those memories back to me. Always 2.27am.

In 1992, my Dad died. He had a heart attack. It was unexpected and he died at home in the night.

For the rest of her life my Mum woke every night at the time of his death, 2.27 am.

Waltzing With Zombies.

By

Keith Suddrey.

All my life I've been dancing with and around automata

while making a beautiful collection of words.

Mechanical drudges constructed with trickster art,

token creatures engrossed in vivid games

yet unclear of movements that mirror existence.

Pass through burlesque parodies in petticoats

governed by a desire to be approachable,

when really sitting within their own flayed epiglottis....

....but I never put on my shoes with wire,

or played with puppets in the glasshouse

while pursuing my neighbours with a mangled harmonica,

after suffering a psychological collapse due to stress.

Senses wound tighter than tight,

a kind of Lazarus in a grotesque song

written in past and present tense.

Discourses that converse with extinction,

as dodos leave footprints in The Book Of The Dead

and promise a new procedural for casual violence.

Beginnings and endings with implications,

ready cocked syntax with rhythm and feet.

Trick or Treat.

By

Julie Taylor.

It's Halloween aunt Mabel said a party we must throw

Let's rent a scary haunted house for all our friends to go

So searching on the Internet a scary house she found

With doors that creaked and floors that made a really weird
sound

We'll rent it shouted Mabel this is the kind of place

That's bound to wipe that happy smile off everybody's face

The invites soon were posted to all of Mabel's friends

Requesting to wear fancy dress when everyone attends

Mabel soon got busy with scary decorations

Her sole intent to totally scare her friends and her relations

On hallows eve by 8 o'clock the guests were all outside

Welcome to my scary night aunt Mabel said with pride.

But nothing had prepared her for the real ghosts to attend

Twas going to be a frightening night that seemed to never end

Billy was the first inside declaring it's a scam

Until he saw a floating plate with sarnies filled with ham.

Frankie ran to help his mate he thought he'd worked it out

The plate must be suspended with fishing line no doubt.

The ghost was getting angry so launched the plate at frank

And hit him square between the eyes as to the floor he sank.

Jenny as a pumpkin ran over to assist

The ghost then threw a trifle but luckily he missed.

Jenny thought twas Billy that had the trifle thrown

So lobbed a plate of lobster that hit him with a groan.

The ghost was now amused to see the friends were now at war

And quickly raced at Trev and Jane as they came through the door.

Jane was blaming Trevor for pulling on her hair

So hit him with custard tart you should have heard him swear

Andy in his top hat came marching in to see

What all the fuss was all about as a mango hit his knee

He turned and spotted Mabel who was giggling in the hall

He was sure he'd found the culprit as he launched a huge cheese ball

Mabel tried to dodge it but stumbled over dean

Who'd thought it would be funny to come dressed as a bean.

With all the guests now in the house they heard the front door lock

A ghostly voiced from up the stairs said let the party rock.

As guests climbed out the windows and raced off down the street

A booming voice was heard to shout now that is trick or treat.

The Witch Hunt.

By

Lucy Webb.

They called me a witch.

Among other names, but 'witch' was my favourite.

Whore

Bitch

Slut

Witch

It was rather appropriate on account of it being Halloween, and everything.

I've always loved Halloween.

My thoughts were that the comment came from some old fella who still believed women should stay at home, mending socks or whatever we did before we moved into the twenty first century. Yeah, definitely an old bloke; my generation are much more creative with their insults.

I could see where he was going with it though.

See, witches are scary and manipulative, but they're easy to kill. Chuck a bucket of water over us and watch us melt away, extinguish our voices, our opinions, our existence.

Or tie us to a stake and set fire to us, watch our reputation go up in flames, regardless of our innocence. The witch metaphor was not lost on me.

When the photo first appeared online; a candid shot of myself, eyes glazed and heavy, my breasts exposed, left one annoyingly slightly bigger than the right, I spent hours clicking 'refresh,' examining each comment as it appeared. I started mentally marking the slurs out of ten, highest points for originality and brutality.

I could not remember the photographer who made me an internet sensation. He was a silhouette with a big nose and crooked teeth, features softened by vodka, with a name I did not catch. But it wouldn't matter if I did. I've learnt that wicked men get to hide in the shadows, behind fake profiles and keyboards, whilst witches are chased with pitchforks and fire.

I tried to make a voodoo doll to punish him. I used buttons for eyes and sprayed it with Calvin Klein aftershave. I think that's what he was wearing. I stuck in three pins: one in each eye, and one in the crotch. I hope he felt it, but my sewing skills aren't up to much.

More comments appeared by the minute. They said I was asking for it. I deserved this. They would give me a good seeing to, if they ever saw me in person. I'd become a warning for other girls; don't be as stupid as me, don't drink as much, don't dress so revealing, don't wear lipstick that bright.

I liked that lipstick. I pouted in the mirror as I applied it again.

All the words came at me like little needles jabbing into my skin. I felt like the insults were being tattooed across my body for everyone to see. But the thing with tattoos is that the pain starts to ease after a minute or two and just becomes an annoying buzz instead of a sharp sting.

People asked me if I felt ashamed of myself, and I did at first. It was a painful thud that started low in my stomach, and slowly crept through my bones, causing me to curl up and wish I could disappear.

I did not know that I could feel that my whole body was freezing, but also at the same time, scorching hot, like someone had doused me in petrol and set me alight.

But the shame quickly evolved into anger. Now, whenever I saw the photograph, my body felt hot, but for a different reason. I wanted revenge.

Life would be easier if I really was a witch. I would conjure up a plague with my fury alone, cast spells by reciting the words of the women who came before me. I would mix up potions in a cauldron under a full moon; a dash of wolf whistles, the little finger of a hand that liked to

165

roam too much, a sprinkle of sexual harassment. The mixture would be called 'Your Own Medicine.'

At least Halloween allowed me to pretend, if only for a night. I could be someone else, someone powerful who wasn't afraid of the dark. The monsters were no longer boogeymen who lived under the bed; they were Anonymous751, Supertroll69 and Devilman666, online ghosts that hid behind keyboards and enjoyed spreading their poison across the web.

I slipped on a black dress that hugged my figure and made the most of my wonky breasts. Fishnet tights and black stiletto boots highlighted the paleness of my legs. As the teen movies stated, tonight we were allowed to dress however we wanted and not be called out for it. The finishing touch was of course, a black hat.

Long gone was the hooked, plastic nose attached to my face with a string of elastic, the green face paint and cloak made from a bin liner. Witches weren't old hags anymore, frightening and tempting the beautiful with apples and promise of true love. Now witches could be young, mysterious, manipulative and that was terrifying. Maybe that was why witches are hated so much.

We've all read the stories in the newspapers. A red headed prince who married a witch and fell under her spell. A president who raged and worried the 'wicked witch of the left' would steal his power. The girl who drank too much at a party and woke up, topless and alone.

I glanced in the mirror one last time before collecting my bag and keys.

I was heading back to where it had all started. Another party, more alcohol, maybe another girl whose life was about to be destroyed.

Maybe the photographer was there again, dressed as the devil and as charming as a snake. Maybe he would recognise me, feel a smidge of guilt. Maybe he would offer me another drink, with a sprinkle of roofie. That was his potion.

I could hear the faint throb of noughties dance music from across the street. The last time I was down here, I couldn't find my bra and my tongue was dry and sour with dehydration.

I saw the house. I recognised the unkempt front garden, weeds creeping through cracks in the concrete and broken glass shimmering under the moonlight. I had entered and left this house two different people.

That morning was a strange one.

I had woken naked from the waist up, not remembering undressing. I had experienced the anxiety that always seems to come from a hangover before, but nothing compared to this. Not knowing whose hands had been on my body the night before. Not knowing if they had explored the most intimate parts of myself, whilst I lay unconscious on a stranger's bed.

Then stumbling home to take a hot shower and drink a gallon of black coffee.

I remember plugging my phone in because it had run out of charge the night before.

Annoyingly, because of this, I had to shower in silence.

I wish I had savoured that shower more. I could keep telling myself that nothing had happened the night previous, drive down the panic that was slowly creeping up my body. I was forcing unwanted images out of my head by mentally deciding what I was going to eat for breakfast. I scrubbed my skin a little harder, but only to get rid of the smell of smoke and booze, not because someone's dirty hands had been all over me the night before. No, definitely not. That sort of stuff doesn't happen to girls like me.

Then I saw that my phone had fourteen text messages and twelve notifications and that was the beginning.

The house where my photoshoot had taken place was just brick and cement, nothing out of the ordinary. It was missing one of its numbers; the paint glaringly white with an outline of the number 'six' where the ceramic plaque once hung. I had found the party that night by following a trail of online breadcrumbs but instead of gingerbread and candy, I had found jelly shots and sickly, sweet cocktails.

I was like a greedy child, drinking anything and everything that was handed to me. However, this time, I was coming back as the witch.

A huddle of men lingered outside, clutching cigarettes and tins of alcohol. They were loudly discussing the football and what girl they were going to shag that night.

Their costumes did not impress much. Dressing up for Halloween meant wearing what they did normally, and purchasing a cheap, plastic mask from the quid shop. One of them must have been feeling a little more creative as he had smeared fake blood around his mouth and was donning plastic fangs.

I spotted the last few trick or treaters being ushered away from the riff raff by parents. I felt envious of the children. I longed for the days when the scariest thing to me was the dark, and not the threat of being followed too closely by strange men in cars. Or being shouted and sworn at because I dared wear shorts on a hot day. Or having a stranger's phone shoved under my skirt on a busy bus.

I felt the fury build within in me once again, and marched towards the open door. I felt the eyes of the men follow me, smirks plastering their faces as they recognised me. One of them wolf whistled.

I hated them. I hated that they would never know the true fear of being a woman. The need to clench keys between fingers when walking down an empty street, just in case we needed them for self-defence. Having to pretend to have a boyfriend in a club just to get someone to leave us alone.

Not all men, they say.

Well, not all witches have to burn.

I squeezed my way through crowds of people, all drunk and having a good time. The kitchen was stocked up with booze, and I found a lukewarm, unopened beer. I poured half of it into an unsuspecting house plant. I needed to be sober for this. My shoes were high enough to convince everyone that I was pissed.

I saw him in the kitchen, flirting with a girl dressed in a skin-tight cat suit and wearing kitten ears. I knew it was him, remembered the sharpness of his cheekbones, the glint in his eyes. I remembered his face the way you remember an old pop song you haven't heard since you were ten. A couple of beats and then all the lyrics come flooding back.

I tilted my hat down and pretended to sip my drink. I watched him touch her arm as she giggled, take his phone out to show her something. The phone may as well have been the match that lit the pyre I was tied to.

The witch hunt was about to come to an end.

It was time to become the hunter.

The Scarecrow.

By

Victoria Hydes.

I t's watching me again," Georgia wavered as she sipped on the steaming cup of tea wrapped up comfortably in her hands, her agitated foot tapping lightly against the stone tiles beneath her.

"Not this again," Paul groaned as he glanced up from his laptop to see her back was once again turned to him, her gaze instead fixated on the fields that made up their new back yard. It had been this way ever since they'd moved in three weeks ago and he was honestly surprised she hadn't dropped it by now.

"Come on, even you have to admit it's creepy, right?" she replied with pleading eyes as she finally turned to face him.

"It's just a scarecrow Babe. Not like it can hurt you or anything. Just come away from the window and try not to think about it." He shook his head as he realised she wouldn't be so easily settled and pushed himself to his feet, the chair legs scraping as he did so. He wandered around the weathered dining table, gently wrapping his arms around her waist and planting a soft kiss on her forehead that put her instantly at ease.

"Careful, I'm carrying tea," she murmured, not actually minding his attempts at affection in the slightest. Deep down she knew he was right, that she was just being silly, but that didn't change the fact she got chills every time she passed by that kitchen window. Maybe it was the fact that her idea of a scarecrow was a crudely built straw figure with a smiling face and colourful overalls, not something straight from a horror movie, its expression manic and bearing what looked suspiciously like real rotten teeth, its base clothed in a ragged black cloak faded by its constant exposure to the sunlight.

Paul backed off slightly so she could place the mug down safely on the side, before taking the opportunity to reach for her still-warm hand and guide her out of view of the figure.

"Do you think you could maybe take it down?" she asked. "I thought I'd get used to it but I just can't. It's not like either of us are planning to grow anything out there and besides, I've already seen plenty of birds lingering regardless."

"You heard what the neighbours said, the estate agents too. We can make any renovations we like but under no circumstances are we to ever remove that scarecrow. They must have a good reason for saying that."

"But what harm can it possibly do? You said it yourself, it's not like it can hurt us."

"The last thing we want is to make enemies before we even have any friends. Maybe if we just cover it with a cloth or something-"

"You know what, forget I said anything," she sighed, throwing her arms up in frustration as she slipped from his grasp and sidled past him. "I'm going to take a bath."

Paul watched after her sadly, before moving to the window to take another look for himself. The way it seemed to be watching their every move was somewhat unnerving – he didn't dispute that – but at the end of the day it was still just some embellished wood and rags. He made a mental note to grab one of the spare bed sheets. At least that should somewhat ease her conscience.

Heading through to the bedroom cupboard where they kept their spare linen, he hesitated outside the bathroom door, curious about the deafening silence. Georgia had a habit of singing to herself in the bath, and he couldn't hear any running water either.

"Babe?"

No response.

Frowning, he cautiously eased open the door, bracing himself for the carnage she might throw at him for interrupting her unannounced. No bathwater; no Georgia; no signs of life anywhere.

"Babe?" he called out again as he padded back out onto the landing. "You up here?"

Suddenly concerned he hurried downstairs, peering around every doorway and growing increasingly anxious when she still failed to materialise. Finally, he reached the back door, yanking it open and wrapping an arm around his body as a brisk breeze whipped through his shirt. That was when he saw her, back once again turned, a long, dirt-covered post gripped tightly in her shaking hand.

"Georgia..." he warned, approaching her slowly. "What are you doing?"

"Well, you clearly weren't man enough to do it so I figured I'd just get the job done myself. This is my house and I want this thing gone. Screw tradition. Nothing more than silly folktales, those stories."

Paul flinched slightly as she tossed it aside, before roughly wiping off her hands on her jeans and flashing him a satisfied smirk.

"Dinner?" she offered sweetly as she waltzed past him, as though a huge weight had just been lifted.

"Sure," Paul wavered, turning back to where the scarecrow now lay face-down on the ground beside a gaping hole and a small mound of damp soil. He briefly considered restoring it, before shaking his head and following meekly after her instead. He wasn't traditionally the superstitious type, but he couldn't help having a bad feeling about this.

Georgia tossed and turned, unable to settle. It was only when she accidentally kicked Paul, who let out a faint yelp in his sleep, that she was stirred awake. She lay back for a few moments in a cold sweat, wondering where the sudden draft might be coming from. She gazed around the room through hazy eyes. Had she forgotten to close the window or something? No, that was firmly sealed. Slipping out of bed she shuffled around the room, feeling for furniture as her eyes slowly adjusted to the blackness that surrounded them. She cursed under her breath as she stubbed her toe against the dresser, casting an anxious glance at Paul to make sure she hadn't woken him. Turning her attention back to the path ahead of her she finally realised what was wrong.

They never left the bedroom door open, ever, and she was sure she remembered Paul closing it behind them that night because he'd joked about keeping the monsters out. A part of her wanted to simply close it again and clamber back into the comforting embrace of their duvet, but she was now wide awake and growing increasingly restless. Reaching for Paul's nearby phone to use as a torch she peered around the doorframe, before wandering through the hall and down the stairs, where she noticed the faint glow of a light. Her heart pounded faster and faster as she approached the kitchen, a sharp shiver coursing down her spine when her eyes rested on the open back door. She edged forwards, her breathing heavy as she eased it closed and carefully turned the key in the lock. She turned back in slight relief, but it was short lived.

Paul shot upright as he heard her scream, the sound echoing throughout the whole house. Jolting automatically out of bed he stumbled over his carelessly discarded shoes, crashing into his side-table and wincing as his leg made contact with the corner. That would bruise for sure. He awkwardly flicked the light switch, recoiling slightly with his arm raised to shield his burning eyes. Regaining his composure, he limped out of the room, freezing when he reached the top of the stairs and looked down to see a shadowy silhouette that certainly didn't resemble his fiancée.

Suitably afraid he initially backed up to consider his next move carefully, when he heard hammering on the front door. Taking a deep breath, he instinctively reached for his childhood footballing trophy on the unit beside him, brandishing it like a bat despite having very little confidence in its ability to defend him should he be faced with some kind of armed intruder. Maybe it was just the neighbours wondering where the scarecrow had gone. That had to be it, surely.

Trying his hardest to block out his fears he began his descent, one small step at a time, each a little more deliberate than the last. At the very least he had to find Georgia, even if they ultimately had to flee for safety. He briefly noticed her lying across the kitchen floor, unmoving, and he was about to check on her when the knocking sounded again. Letting out an exasperated groan he moved instead to the door, relaxing only slightly when he recognised their visitor as the elderly man from a few doors down the road.

"Thank goodness," he breathed. "I need your help. It's Georgia, she-"

"Where is it?" the man hissed, not sparing a single second for pleasantries.

"W-where's what?"

"You know what."

"My fiancée... she, she was scared and..."

"WHERE IS IT?"

"In the shed."

"Then what are you bloody waiting for? Put it back, now, before you get us all killed!"

Paul was about to respond when the man slipped away into the shadows, leaving him standing on a deserted doorstep. After overcoming his momentary shock he suddenly remembered Georgia and raced back down the hall towards the kitchen, skidding to his knees beside the spot where she lay. He shook her limp body a couple of times, his panic rising to even greater heights when she failed to respond.

He considered calling for help, but judging by the old man's reaction he doubted anyone would come. He shook her again, willing her to wake, stopping only as he felt an unfamiliar chill and watched his arm hairs stand on their ends. Turning slowly, he met with piercing red eyes and had to remind himself to keep breathing. Backing up automatically he couldn't take his own eyes off them. He didn't know what this thing standing before him was, but it certainly wasn't human. He gulped as it raised what looked like an arm minus the muscle, with razor-sharp talons for fingers. He wanted to scream but no sound left his mouth. Instead he simply stood, stunned, frozen to the spot. Only when it lunged towards him did his adrenaline finally kick in, allowing him to leap back just in time and turn in the direction of the back door. Fumbling with the key through sweaty palms he forced it open, almost pulling it off its hinges, before taking off at a determined run across the back yard.

"I told you we shouldn't have messed with that thing," he grumbled under his breath, barely registering the way the damp mud seeped between his bare toes, or the roughness of the loose stones that dug into the soles of his feet. He couldn't tell if the creature was following him, but he didn't dare look back to check.

Barrelling into the shed he rummaged frantically in an attempt to dislodge the still mostly assembled scarecrow from the spot where he'd wedged it safely behind some spare boxes. A couple of involuntary tears prickled in the corners of his eyes as he heard strained breathing from directly behind him and felt an icy chill brush over the back of his neck. He was trapped and there was nowhere left to hide. Preparing for the worst, he turned, eyes screwed shut in pure terror, but he was most surprised when nothing happened. Finally chancing a peek with one eye he noticed the creature shrinking back, almost as though it was now the one that was afraid. Paul frowned as his eyes rested briefly on the stick in his hand. Holding it proudly up before him he took a few cautious steps forwards, amazed to see the creature continuing to back off at the same pace.

His confidence growing, he continued towards the spot where it used to stand, triumphantly forcing it back into the ground with ease and hastily packing the dirt back around its base with his foot to secure it in place. He watched in awe as the creature let out a shrill wail, before fading back into the shadows. He could feel his chest constrict as he attempted to regulate his breathing again, his gaze now turned to the same ominous shadows rising and fading all around him from the surrounding streets.

Then quiet. Stillness. Just like any ordinary night.

He turned his attention back to the scarecrow, which grinned its familiarly menacing grin. What had just happened? Had it all been some strange dream or a trick of the imagination, or had that thing really been there in his house?

"What did we tell you?" the man from before growled as he appeared at the fence, panting. "You don't move the scarecrow. Ever!"

"What was that?"

179

"That was what the scarecrow keeps at bay. They've haunted our town for centuries now, and this thing seems to be the only way of warding them off. Don't ask me why. It was my father who told me the tale, and his father before him. Now, your girl, where is she?"

"God, that's right," he exclaimed, turning quickly and dashing back into to the house, ignoring the man's calls after him. Returning to her side he once again scooped Georgia up into his arms, holding her close. "Please, wake up," he begged.

"Step back," the man demanded from the doorway. Paul turned, his eyes widening as he realised he was now pointing a shotgun right at them.

"Whoa, what gives?" he urged, throwing his arms up in surrender. "We're sorry, ok?"

"I said step back."

"But-"

"If you want to live, step away from the girl."

"What are you going to do to her?"

"I'm sorry, but there's no other way. She's one of them now."

Paul shook his head, determined to stand his ground despite his true desire to simply break down. He and the man locked eyes, considering one another carefully. After what felt like an eternity, Georgia began to stir, catching

Paul's attention. He started to smile but hesitated when her eyes opened and he realised they were now as red as the monster's, and that her teeth were sharpened as she smiled that challenging smile he'd once got such a thrill out of seeing. His eyes moved to her looming hand, now tipped with those same crooked talons that were sure to haunt his dreams for years to come. He instinctively edged away, flinching as the distinctive blast of the gunshot rang through his ears without any further warning. Paralysed with shock and unable to watch as her blood seeped into the cracks between the tiles, he slumped back, head in his hands, and finally allowed himself to cry.

He felt the man's hand firmly grip his shoulder and glanced up. His fierce demeanour had been replaced by a sympathetic and knowing smile, and Paul could see in his eyes that this wasn't his first time dealing with these things.

"Come on," he coaxed, rising from his crouching position beside Paul and offering his hand, "Where do you keep your liquor? I think we could use a drink, don't you?"

Several hours later Paul found himself gazing idly out the kitchen window, a still untouched glass of whiskey gripped firmly in his quaking hand while his restless foot tapped on repeat, much like Georgia's had done less than twenty-four hours prior. He couldn't take his eyes off her favourite mug, resting between some unwashed plates by the sink, the remains of her leftover tea still swimming miserably in the bottom, ice cold. He breathed deeply to settle the growing lump in his throat and glanced up, locking eyes with those of the scarecrow that had saved his life. He was sure he noticed a concentrated breeze rippling through its cloak, but to his relief those piercing red eyes didn't follow. Even so, he'd never be able to look at that yard the same way again, just like he'd no longer be able to relax in the comfort of this kitchen without seeing the contorted body of what remained of the woman he'd once dreamed of spending his life with. They never should have moved here. He should have listened to her.

Throwing some essentials into a large holdall he marched outside, unlocking his car as he approached. He wasn't sure where he'd go or whether he should really be driving in his condition, but what he was certain of was that he couldn't stay in that house, not anymore. He stuck his key in the ignition and breathed deeply as the engine roared to life and some pop song he didn't recognise blared from the radio. He pulled out slowly, not looking back.

Old Clee.

By

Pauline Seawards.

Rooks make shadows and seagulls soar,

yew tree path leads to a heavy, locked door.

Skeleton tree beckons with crooked branches

The church tower is over a thousand years old.

Lichen camouflages crumbling grave-stones.

Deeply chiselled names make a silent spell.

Centuries have passed since Amos Appleyard

called out to Annie, his beloved wife.

Yet there is so much life here

beetles scuttle in grass, worms turn underground

a laurel bush is a chorus of sparrows.

And tonight at Halloween a Gothy crew will gather

black lace, black leather and black eyeliner

drink to the moon with cans of cider

Wills and Wiles.

By

Grace King.

My Granddad always told me not to leave my life up to fate. Fate was just other people making decisions for you. And he certainly didn't like Halloween.

"Quick, close the door!" A gloomy-eyed girl, in her late teens, bustled past me as she tugged at my coat. A back-draft of wind thrust burnt-up leaves over my scuffed shoes as she pressed it shut.

"Who were you running from?" The girl asked, kneeling to the coffee shop floor.

"Sorry, what?" I asked.

"I was talking to Gladroid," she said. I strained to see over her shoulder but she stood up and opened her palm.

"Oh, good lord." I laughed and forcibly kept my feet still.

"He's harmless." Gloomy Girl caught me with her eyes. The orange-striped tarantula stretched its legs in her hand.

"That can't have wandered in on its own," I threw a sceptical eye at the busy city centre.

"He's mine, and essential this time of year," she said, shrugging into the tips of her brown hair, "a real good judge of character." The look she gave it was the same burst of excitement I gave my professional drawing pens on my birthday.

"What does he think of—

"Carica-Kai!" My eyebrows raised with the chirpy call that came from Dana on the other side of the room. Gloomy Girl's face ricocheted like a confused woodpecker as her attention flew to the barista behind the counter. My cheeks hugged my eyes, "I'm Kai, and that's my course-mate, Dana. This Café is named after her mum, Sadie. She went missing when Dana was a child," I said. Gloomy girl put her ear close to the spider without responding to me, and I cleared my throat. "Anyway, I best go, as no doubt, she'll have already started making my order."

"See you around," Gloomy Girl said and cocooned the spider with her body as she hurried away. My stomach dropped as I gaped after her.

"That's £2.65, Carica-Kai," Dana shouted as her last customer walked away. I hustled over to collect my cappuccino, smiling at the cinnamon dusting.

"Will you be going out tonight?" Dana flashed me a Cheshire-cat grin as I sucked up the spicy foam.

"I plan to," I said as she put my change on the counter. I started picking it up but she stroked my hand with her fingers. Her long nails accidentally dragged across my skin, and I pulled my hand back.

"Can't wait to see your costume."

"I'm not dressing up this year."

"Then you'll go perfectly with my outfit," her lip ring glinted as she spoke. "I'll be a vampire searching for the fresh blood of men."

"Very fitting," I said and placed the lid on my takeaway cup. "See you later!"

Hoping to have another run in with Gloomy Girl, I made a move towards the exit but my eyes found her at a table with her friends. Her spider glided along her arm and I sighed, inhaling the rich coffee aroma.

I reached for the door handle but my knuckles thudded against the metal as I realized my hand was already full. I unfolded my fingers to find an old penny and pealed back my top lip. That wasn't there before. A cold gust tunnelled down my throat as I slid it into my pocket and yanked the door open.

Hungry air clawed at my neck and I tucked my chin into my scarf as I entered the golden streets. It wasn't that I didn't like Halloween, if it was all in good fun, but some people fetishized poltergeists, witches and zombies; all those creations that defied natural laws. It just made me uncomfortable. I was more of a spring person; there's a natural order of things and the magic was in the peace it brought.

I settled down on a cold bench and pulled out my sketchbook to draw the spider from earlier. I was imagining it with the same gloomy eyes as its owner, which was easy to achieve in this smoky backdrop. As I got to its legs, I couldn't help drawing claws, shuddering from the memory of Dana's black nails.

"Any change please?" a sorry voice, both quiet and loud, made me drop my drawing pen. A homeless man, with bags under his silver eyes patted his holey trousers. He smiled when he saw my sketchbook and his moony gaze connected with mine. It reminded me of Grandad's joy when he'd first seen my work.

"Yes, course," I fumbled through my pockets, only to realize my hand was already wrapped around that penny again. I was keen to be rid of it but I couldn't just give him that. I opened my bag and dug out a few quid.

"Here," I said, but his moony eyes darkened as if clouds had passed over them.

He bowed his head and walked away. I watched him go and let the breeze pale my skin. High heels sounded behind me and I turned around as a fog approached the back of my bench. A shot of black appeared in the corner of my eye and I twisted my head to see a large dog hurtling towards Moony Man.

I jumped to my feet to warn him but my voice halted. It was like watching in slow motion as, in that split second, I worried about alerting the dog's attention to me. Wind whistled in my ears as I snapped myself out of it and I yelled for him to watch out. He didn't hear me. Fog swirled around his ankles as the dog came close. "Look out!" I cried, but the canine clamped its teeth into Moony Man's side. He stumbled to the ground as the dog mounted him.

"That's the best thing I've seen in ages," a voice nicked my ears and my head jerked to the side. A blond woman stood smiling at me and I writhed. I looked again at the scene but it was completely swallowed up by fog.

"Fuck!"

I ran forwards but the woman grabbed my arm.

"Hey, wait!" I tried to shake her off. "My name's Felicity," she said and I escaped her grip but she circled in front of me. "I'm an art scout for the city."

My eyes widened. "We need to call an ambulance! that man's hurt!"

The beaming woman followed my gaze with two slow blinks. "What man?" she said. And she was right. When the air cleared, there was no sign of the dog or Moony Man.

"Didn't you see that dog attack?"

"No, but the fellow can't be too hurt if he's already scampered off," her voice scraped my bones like a bike in need of oiling. "Listen, I love your sketch, it's very Freudian."

"What?"

"Maybe we could come to an arrangement where you make five of this kind of thing," she waved her hand over my sketchbook, "for an upcoming exhibition. I'll pay you £150 for each piece."

"What?" I asked again, feeling an odd sense of this not being real.

"I need them by the end of November," she said, digging into her purse and pulling out her card.

I peered around the deserted area again as shivers crawled up my arms like tarantulas.

High heels broke my trance and I realized the lady was leaving. I checked her feet but she was wearing Uggs.

"Wait," I said, scratching my eyebrows, "why did you say Freudian?"

"The way the spider's fur looks soft, yet it has claws. It reminds me of the perils of sex. Something repulsive can also be seductive, and what promises us comfort can also cause us deep, psychological pain." She dangled her fingers over my art again, "so subtle."

"Right," I raised my eyebrows, "good catch."

"Anyway, give me a call...?"

"Kai."

"Fabulous." She scurried away.

Stuffing the card in my pocket, I was weirdly aware that the old penny was no longer there. Dana would freak out if she knew about the night I was having.

**

My shoes padded soundlessly as I searched for Moony Man. Thirty feet away was another bench but I couldn't see it clearly through the mist. As I got closer, I realized a man was sitting there.

"Excuse me," I said, sprinting towards him, "did you see an injured man pass by?" I clutched my hips as I stopped to catch my breath.

"Sorry, I didn't see anyone." He didn't even glance up and it was only then that I noticed the small box in his hand. He was turning it over and over.

"Are you sure? He must have come by here."

"I'm pretty sure, seen as my girlfriend just dumped me and I've been waiting for her to come back." The man opened the box to reveal a shimmering ring, "what a fool I've been." He stood up and finally looked at me. Although the night around my vision was weaving thick, blurry air, there was no mistaking the change that happened in his eyes. His intense, dark irises stretched and bleached as though someone had switched a light on inside. He almost looked mesmerised.

"Here, I want you to have this," he stuffed the box into my hand.

"What are you doing?" I tried to give it back but he held up his hands.

"I just know it's meant for you," he said and bolted away.

What the hell?

As I stood there, heart clawing at my chest, I thought about how Dana would revel in this madness.

Without knowing what else to do, I slid the box into my pocket and swayed with the skittering lamp lights.

**

My search was leading nowhere. No dog-attack victims had been admitted to hospital and no-one had sighted Moony Man.

My phone said it was ten to ten. Dana would be finishing work at half past and I hadn't even gone home to shower or have dinner yet. I didn't want to end my search but it was as if the tragedy had never happened.

Punching my fist into my other hand, I caught sight of a taxi pulling up beside me.

I gritted my teeth and paced around, avoiding eye contact with the driver. The back door opened and sad, black-framed eyes peered up at me.

Gloomy Girl.

She was dressed as a witch in a puffed-out skirt and laced top. She waved off the taxi driver but he stayed put, staring at me like I was a walking, talking pumpkin.

"Hey kid! Something tells me you need a ride. If you're on my way home, which is in Beeston, then this one won't cost you," he said. Gloomy girl gawked at me and recognition illuminated her eyes.

"No thanks, have a nice night!" I called back, hoping my cheeks weren't blotting pink.

"You too, son. I wish you the very best." He drove away.

"Do you know him?" Gloomy girl approached me as she placed a bent-tipped hat on her now purple, glittering hair. I held my breath as she came closer, afraid that her eyes would become just as joyfully-vacant as the rest of the population tonight. Thankfully, her gloom held.

"Sorry," I said, aware of how strange I must seem scanning her. "No, I don't know any taxi drivers."

"He took a shine to you like a pretty penny."

"What did you just say?" I spread my fingers in my penniless pockets.

"Are you ok? You look spooked."

"I'm having a strange night. Do you... are you feeling generous at all, right now?" I peered closely at her again and she leaned back.

"If you needed money to get somewhere, you should have taken the taxi," she said and treaded away.

"It's just people have been treating me like a God all night. And you're the first person to treat me like a stranger," I raised my voice and she turned around.

"You're the boy from Sadie's earlier, aren't you?"

"Yes, I'm Kai."

"My spider, Gladroid, liked you," she said as if I'd passed a background check.

"You never gave me your name," I said, not feeling glad my luck might have run out with her.

"I'm May." She fiddled with the pendent around her neck as her eyes went to some far off distance. "Have people been acting like that taxi driver to you all night?"

"Yes, even a cat started massaging my feet earlier when I was sat down. Everyone's been ogling me."

"I don't know whether to tell you... or if you'd believe me..."

"What?"

"I brought Gladroid out because I don't trust people on Halloween. The Veil's so weak, evil can be summoned. I wear protection charms so I fall for no illusions," she said and I stepped back. She was a fetishist.

Her neck began to shrink into her shoulders so I threw her an encouraging nod.

"I'm an Earth Witch, and I like to practice seeing auras and spells. If you let me, I can try and see if there's any fuzzy lights around your aura? before I go and meet my friends," she added. "It's possible someone's put a spell on you, and that's why I'm not falling for it, because of my protections." She gripped her pendent tighter.

After a few seconds, I realized it was my turn to talk.

"I feel like I'm being pranked." My toes curled into my shoes. "Tell me now if you're messing with me." I narrowed my eyes. I didn't care how pleasing her voice was,

I didn't know her. And I wasn't about to fall for some hoodoo bullshit.

"Never mind," she said, and mumbled something stabbing that I couldn't catch. I heard the clanking of heels as she stormed away.

"Wait, please," I rushed after her, taking in her flat, black shoes. "I'm sorry. I'm having a weird night and it's hard for me to believe…" I couldn't forgive myself if I was gullible to this.

May's posture melted, "I understand. It's not a joke. I wouldn't mess with people's minds like that," she said. Something blocked up my throat and I turned my face away.

"My school friends used to trick me into believing in this kind of stuff. I developed night terrors," I admitted. "They spread rumours about me, but my Grandad helped me get over it by thinking more logically."

"He sounds like a good man. But I would never be as cruel as your friends," May said.

How could I trust what she was saying? Plenty of people would make an oath like that part of their joke.

Tension rested in my stomach, but one more look at her kind, doll-like face made the feeling go away.

"Will you check my aura?" My teeth latched together.

May nodded and audibly took in three deep breaths and exhaled them like blossom falling from a branch.

**

"I see an entity attached to you." May's eyes darted above my head. She closed them and curled down her lips. "It's split in half. You have the tail-end while someone else has the head." I watched her pupils moving behind her lids. "You're getting good luck, but they're paying for it," she said as her breath ruptured.

I was still checking for signs she was kidding.

May's eyes fluttered open as she pivoted her relaxed stare towards me.

"Someone gave you this entity. It was dormant at first, but you made it active."

"How?"

May squinted hard and then shook her head. "I've lost my focus," she said but the way her fingers rubbed together made my spine straighten.

"Who'd want me to be happy at the expense of someone else?" If it was true.

May tapped her foot and looked at the ground.

"Do you have any idea who the other person might be?"

I realized what May's fingers reminded me of and I pulled my hand from my pocket.

"I gave a penny to a homeless man. Everything changed after that. He got attacked by a stray dog and disappeared."

"We need to find him. Now."

"I don't know where he went."

"There was a chequered floor beneath the other half of the entity I saw."

"In front of the library there's a life-size chessboard," I said and grabbed her hand to run.

**

Moony Man was lying face down when we arrived out of breath. Blood pooled around him on the library steps. His t-shirt was ripped apart, revealing deep gashes all over his body. May dialled for an ambulance as I knelt beside him and checked for a pulse. His neck rolled against the tips of my fingers and I relaxed.

"I'm sorry," I said, and opened his hand. Stuck to his palm like wet tissue on a grungy bathroom wall, was the penny, and I took it.

"We need to destroy that," May said, hanging up the phone.

"I know. I just didn't want him to keep the bad luck in case it stopped help from coming."

"An ambulance is on the way," she said. "You're a good person, Kai. Gladroid's never wrong."

I looked up at her tiny silhouette and my body softened like clean fur.

"If Gladroid approved of me, then why did you dash away from me at Sadie's?"

"He didn't like your friend. I thought it best to avoid you because of association."

"Dana? She's not shady or anything. She's just alternative."

"I trust Gladroid's opinion, Kai. Otherwise I wouldn't be helping you."

A siren broke our tension and I stood up.

"You should go and destroy the penny. If you have bad luck now, you might get accused of doing this," she gestured to the ill-fated man.

"You couldn't see who cast the spell when you were studying my aura?" I asked, fighting the rush to leave. I didn't have her number and I worried I'd never see her again.

"You might know. Subconsciously they've tied their soul to yours, while the spell is in effect," she spilled out her words like ink. "There might be traces."

Fog glided up from behind May's skirt and beside her own round face, there formed a fleshy, disembodied head. A growing hole ate its way across a point below its bulging eyes, and it swooped past May towards me. It smacked into my shoulder like a bowling ball and I fell to the ground, grazing my bag and arms against the concrete. A sharp pinch spliced my voice as the head released its teeth from my skin.

"It's you isn't it," I said to May. My chest felt emptied after seeing how the head went nowhere near her. "Stop the spell!" I yelled as spit stuck to my lips.

The skinless head flew towards me again but I kicked it back.

"Kai," May stepped forward but I propelled myself up and scarpered.

**

May must have put the penny in my pocket when she'd passed me at Sadie's. And she's been in my thoughts all night which must have been the traces.

My legs gave way when I rounded the back of the large building. I hid behind some bins and rang Dana.

"Hey, I've just finished my shift."

"Dana you need to come get me. I'm at the back of the Library." I hung up and pulled out the penny. Letting it fall to the black floor, I stomped on it before realizing that wouldn't destroy it. Sweat dribbled down my forehead as a sandpapery voice cut through the night, "Oi!" it said and I cursed.

**

Dana pulled up in a taxi two minutes too late.

I limped towards her and she swathed me into a hug. I rested against her like she was a blanket but the tighter I held her, the more it felt like nails were raking over my skin. She drew away and looked me over.

"I was joking when I told you I wanted the fresh blood of men." She cackled and I cringed.

"A mugger stabbed me after he took my bag and a stupid ring. But it doesn't matter. We need to destroy this penny," I said, feeling my lungs dampen from my hot breath. I produced the old coin in my shaking hand.

"So, you finally believe in magic."

Although it was dark in the alleyway, Dana's teeth glinted, revealing a vampiric grin. I nearly collapsed with distraught.

"Dana, I know you have an urge to not help me but that's because of a spell."

"Oh, I know what's going on, Carica-Kai. I'm the one who cast it."

Fog thickened around us.

"You did this?"

Shadows taunted my eyes as I scanned the haze for any emerging heads.

"I was sick of being dismissed by you. You thought I was some deluded creep, didn't you?"

"Dana, what the f—"

"So now that you've realized your grave error. I'll break the spell for a price," she said. "I want the kiss you've been denying me all year because you thought I was crazy."

"You don't think you are?"

"Kai!" May's distant voice carried over the fog.

"May?"

"I can't get through."

My searching eyes stopped when the skull finally showed itself.

"This isn't real. It's a vile, heartless prank!"

"You're killing me, Kai!" Dana's sigh turned into a laugh.

The skinless head barrelled towards my bleeding leg and I staggered. But before it could bite me, a glittery fist punched it away.

May laced her fingers through mine. "It's alright, Kai, even though it's real," she said and I noticed her pendent was gone.

"How can this horror be real?"

"Where there's evil, there's always good," she said and she batted away the attacking head again. "We need to pray." May squeezed my hand, and for the first time in a long time, I did.

Grandad...

It may be stupid to assume you'd hear this...

It's not what you taught me to believe. But I think you're listening.

I need your help.

Please!

You need to make a choice, Kai.

The ghost of Grandad's voice overpowered the raised threats that Dana was hurling at May and I. A dusty breeze hit my back pocket and a glow flicked on in my eyes. Reaching behind my back, I yanked my pen loose and drew the Christian Cross on May's arm.

"A protection charm," she said. I did the same to myself. The skinless head came diving again but this time it froze in mid-air. The fog began to thin and we saw our way out. I shoved into Dana as we fled, dumping the coin into her costume's hood.

"Dana's got the penny," I told May once we were free.

"Then the spell has nowhere to go."

The ringing sound of heels clicking against pavement finally showed their offender. Two black shoes with dismembered feet trapsed behind Dana, pausing just below the floating head. A body forged between them, then flesh, and then long, black hair. Dana's face stripped back as she whined.

"Mum?"

The woman leaned closer and wrapped her hands around Dana's neck. A shallow scream left Dana's throat, sprouting goosebumps along my arms. As Dana's face turned purple, drops of rain disturbed the mist and the view before us dissolved into nothingness.

All that was left was the short clink of copper hitting concrete.

May retrieved her abandoned pendent from the ground, and I stepped forward into the now empty alley, feeling around the barren air.

On the gravel, amidst the pelting rain, was an old penny.

"Leave it," May said, barely audibly over the downpour. "The spell's over. It should rust."

I leaned into her, and she shushed me as she phoned another ambulance.

**

On the ride to the hospital, I thought a lot about choices and fate.

I believe that our choices become smarter, the more aware we are of what's possible in the world. But if we don't want to be aware, then we should be warned.

There'll always be someone out there who is.

The Visitation Copy.

By

Mark Sandford.

What a fool, such is me!

Could I ever overlook to see

The wonder that you'll always be

In life.

A presence that you care to share

With all who open doors and dare

To take your love, with no compare:

To nurture.

Silently you do your worst,

For no one knows that here at first

Your presence lingers close; with bursts

Of emotion.

Oh how I wish that then I knew,

With these tears, a love came true,

And all the time it was surely you that made

Things whole.

The Night I Met Jack.

By

Gemma Owen-Kendall.

It was the night of the full moon during a cold and crisp October evening. I could hear the wolves howling in the distance, there I was standing on my balcony at upon my top floor apartment where I spotted it or him. Some people think that Jack is his name, Jack-a-lantern as he stalks the streets and creeps into homes wearing an orange shaded head mask. He lurks around the darkest of places, the rumours are if you spot him and live, he obviously likes you, I know this as I'm the only one who has lived so far to tell the tale of the night I met Jack.

Jack only appears every October but as soon as the clock strikes midnight on first November he just vanishes. There is not a single trace of him left, the only evidence that has ever been found is the discarded carved pumpkins from a nearby castle ruin. It is believed Jack lives there during the month of October. So tonight of all nights was the moment he took me, there I was standing on my balcony with a glass of cola, at the age of seventeen, my parents did not allow me to drink alcohol. We had some pumpkins recently carved, that were placed on the balcony lit with candles. I was about to go to bed as time was getting on so I blew out the candles when out of nowhere, he suddenly appeared standing on the railing.

He didn't make a sound, I only spotted him as I gazed up and saw the dark silhouette with an orange head. He pointed to the unlit pumpkins but still didn't speak to me. Before I could make a dash for it, he grabbed hold of me. I tried to break free from his clutches but he was too strong for me. I wanted to scream out for help, as I opened my mouth to make a sound, I felt a sharp pain in my neck then everything just went black.

As I came round I was no longer at my parents apartment, I woke up chained to a worn down bed, the metal chains clinked to the bed frames as I tried to break free. There was low lighting in the room, it was mainly by candles scattered round but I could just make out the objects on the wall. What I saw turned my stomach completely inside out, I felt the acidy bile rise up, the more I tried to swallow it down, the more it just burnt my throat. There on the walls hung organs, I couldn't quite tell if they were human or animal but it was enough to make my stomach churn, they appeared to be dried out so could have been stored there for some time, perhaps they were trophies from his victims. Hearts, lungs, stomachs, kidneys and even an intestine hung upon the ceiling like a decoration.

The door to the room swung open and entered a dark shadowy figure, there was no orange mask, the character was just all in black. He stood over me and I could just about make out his eyes upon the candle light, they were dark brown but human looking. I tried to scream again but my throat hurt too much from throwing up. It was a struggle to move with these heavy chains cuffed to me. All I could do now was cry, I didn't want to die, I had lots I wanted to do with my life. After school I plan to go to university and become a writer, I wanted to share me stories with the world. Then a gloved finger started to wipe away my tears, whoever he was didn't want to see me cry. He reached to his left side pocket and pulled out another needle.

"No, please don't hurt me." I managed to finally scramble out the words and plea with him. He moved a finger to my lips and made a hushing sound. If I was going to die he may as well just do it. I laid there limp as the needle jolted into my neck once again and I just waited for my eyes to go heavy and for everything to go black. When I came too I was back on the balcony again, my head feeling fuzzy as I gently sat up. The light of dawn was slowly rising up in the far distance, the temperature overnight had dropped down to just above freezing level. Had I been away from home all night? Did my parents know I had disappeared? Before I moved even further Jack was back on my balcony standing over me, I froze in fear again not knowing what he wanted from me. His orange mask fully covering his identity once again apart from his eyes, those dark human like eyes starring down upon me. He knelt down next to me and lifted up his mask part way to reveal his lip leaning towards my face and planting a kiss upon mine. Surprisingly his kiss was warm and tender, who was Jack-a-lantern? Whoever he was I wanted to be with him.

"You're mine!" he harshly whispered to me, before I could say anything back to him, Jack fled and vanished within a second. I placed my finger tips to my lips trying to sense his kiss and how it felt. I knew I would see Jack again and that I lived to tell the tale of my encounter with him.

The Little Stranger.

By

Tracey Gavan Johnson.

"I want you to believe...to believe in things that you cannot."
Bram Stoker

The battered, little cabin cruiser chugged into Whitby harbour. Had there been anyone around to see, they would in all likelihood, have paid no attention anyway. And anyway, few people were out and about in the fog bound streets that chilly late October night. So there was indeed no one to pay any attention at first when it came to rest, its path blocked by a small flotilla of tiny fishing boats moored up in the middle of the estuary. The gentle waves slapped against its sides as the engine continued to chug, though its way was made impassable. Instead, it gently bumped the wooden prow of the nearest vessel, a small fishing-smack-turned whale watching boat, that by day carried tourists out into the grey and wild North Sea on the lookout for dolphin pods and Minke Whale.

The newcomer was softly batting back and forth blindly, fruitlessly trying to make headway, when at that moment the man and woman, a couple strolled by, chatting quietly, huddled against the cold air, on their way home from The White Horse pub just down the quay.

Drawn by the out of place sound that was breaking the stillness, the woman noticed it first. "What on Earth are they trying to do?" she said, noting the ineffective and pointless butting of the little boat against the others already moored in its path.

Moving closer and peering through the fog, the man said "I don't think anyone's at the wheel".

They walked down a wooden jetty and as they took a closer look, they realised that the boat did indeed look empty of any passengers or crew. The faded name plate read Little Stranger.

"I think we should call the police" said the man.

"Or the coast guard" said the woman "they could have gone overboard".

"Do that will you" said the man, as he clambered aboard. A fisherman himself, he knew exactly where to turn off the engine and steady the boat. The frustrated chugging stopped abruptly, and left only the sound of slapping water to disturb the night air as the woman spoke quickly to the coast guard on her phone.

"Is anyone on board? "she called to her partner in response the same question from the coast guard on the other end of her phone.

"No" replied the man, and then, "hang on though". A pause as he ducked his head inside. "There's someone in the cabin." And after a brief pause for a second look he added "I think they need to send an ambulance."

"Well done to you both" said the police officer some time later when she had heard the full story from them. "It's one of the strangest things I've had to deal with, but I think it's safe to say that your prompt actions have probably saved that young woman's life". The man and woman looked at each other, still unsure what to make of the whole thing.

When he had first seen her, lying there, lifeless in the tiny cabin, the man had indeed thought she was dead. He had helped to pull a dead body from the sea once before and she had that same look. Alabaster pale skin, lips tinged blue and when he had finally managed to shake himself out of his stupor to check for a pulse, her skin was ice cold to the touch. He hadn't found a pulse, but then he wasn't an expert was he? The paramedics had seemed to think she was alive, and she was in the hospital now, indeed alive and apparently in dire need of a blood transfusion. But oh my days. Was she beautiful! Breathtakingly so. He hadn't been able to take his eyes off her, and at first, for a second or two, he had stooped there in the cabin doorway, mesmerised.

No one else was found in the sea that night or in the days which followed, although the Coastguard helicopter went up and the search went on for a week. And no one nor the tiny craft itself were ever reported missing. But the strangest thing, the most peculiar thing of all was what happened next. It was the thing that most baffled the man and haunted him, along with her face, for the rest of his days, and it was this. That after she received her blood transfusion, and was indeed looking much better, the beautiful young woman walked straight out of the hospital and disappeared. No one would ever come to know who she was, for she had not breathed so much as one word to anyone the entire time. And so, try as anyone might to find her, she was never seen again. That is to say, not by a single, living soul.

Praise It.

By

Ants Ambridge.

Alice sat with her back against the wall next to a window, her shallow breathing echoing through the silent house. Beams of light stretched from the cracks in the curtains, illuminating falling specks of dust. With a finger, she pulled back the curtain a fraction, allowing her a line of sight to the street. She only spotted one of them. This looked better than yesterday, when dozens gathered, leaving Alice to fear a breach at any moment.

The figure shuffled onwards, past the empty corner shop and into the distance. She heard the 'fshwee fshwee' sounds of its laboured breaths, struggling to take in the air through the mass of skin drooping from its skull. Some staggered blind, eyes covered with forehead skin, fusing to their cheeks. This one's nose had stretched downwards, the tip dangling below the chin. Flaps covered the rest of its mouth, resulting in the whistling sound. But a single eye remained exposed. Capable of sight, it posed a dire threat.

Not a monster, nor alien, it used to be a human being. Alice pondered what life it had before. Was it a father? Did it remember its family? Its partner? Did any sentience remain in them at all? She closed her eyes, her mind straying back to the start. She often did this; in case she found some answers or solutions to the endless game of cat-and-mouse that she played with these things.

Eighteen months prior, an object plunged through the Earth's atmosphere and splashed down into the North Sea. Very few news outlets covered the story, considering a scientific oddity, nothing more. No ramifications came from the object landing, save for slightly choppier waters in the vicinity for a moment. Still, it offered some scientists value as a curiosity. They'd assumed it to be a meteorite, so a small-scale operation began in order to recover it. With no drama to report, this again to be ignored by all but those with a deep interest in celestial bodies.

Alice had seen an article in a scientific group on Facebook. It spoke of funding issues, and the main take from the story read how the plucky researchers had overcome monetary issues to get a piece of space-rock. What it proved to be didn't enter the narrative. That came later. A picture emerged; another misshapen lump of stone, looking no different from any other. Harmless.

She opened her eyes and took another glance through a sliver of exposed window. A huge silhouette loomed in the distance. Eyes like sparkling jade glowing faintly, twelve by her count. It wasn't harmless anymore. She screwed her eyes and turned away. Every time she looked at the thing, dread clawed through her body from the pits of her stomach. If she tried to scrutinise further, uncontrollable tremors would take over her body and her head would pound. Her thoughts would scramble, and a survival instinct, rather than logic, would force her to turn away. The simplest answer would be to never set eyes on it again, but when she tried to remember details, moments later they would fade from her mind. How should humanity fight back against something they can't gaze upon?

The lab where they took the rock became the subject of a major news report two weeks later. They found a team of scientific researchers dead, flesh looking like it had melted from their faces, and after autopsies, their internal organs ruptured into mush. A survivor, discovered days later, appeared as if he'd suffered a stroke; one half of his face lacking any muscle tone. Looking like a waxwork next to a radiator. After an interview, they quickly dismissed his testimony as trauma induced insanity. He claimed it wasn't a meteorite, but an egg. The thing that emerged had wiped out his comrades without moving. It willed them to die. He'd caught but a glimpse and ran for his life. He warned the public not to rest eyes on it. To do what he did and flee.

His warning had the opposite effect. The prospect of a genuine discovery of alien life became an obsession for some. They made arrests as 'believers' gathered around the lab where the tragedy took place. Online, an investigation took place. Trackers visited the site and followed a trail to a pond nearby. Updates provided in real time by tweets and livestreams. A crowd grew in numbers over the course of an hour. The streams caught manic cries of finding the alien, before the images became distorted into a blurry outline of a shape amid the waters. All communication ceased.

The exact details of what happened at that pond had no record. But all survived, albeit horrifically mutilated. Those still capable of speech made fractured sentences. But all insisting on one thing:

- Praise it.

The news went global, and curious visitors flocked to the pond from overseas, never able to record images, but all suffering the same fate—grotesque deformities and a slim grasp of their sanity. Discussion grew rife online. A war of words between those who begged for people to be cautious, and avoid approaching the thing, and those that insisted that any amount of risk was worth looking at this marvel of their time. Reports of similar rocks emerged from other countries, too. The creature grew easily visible through the trees.

They flooded hospitals in the region with emergencies. Operations to remove skin to allow the patients to breathe became commonplace. Roughly five percent of the visitors to the site died before reaching the hospital, a further three percent during the surgery. All media outlets urged people to stay away as the state called the army in to contain it. They, too, turned by the beast. Arguments circled online that it was to be humankind's saviour, and the media 'drove a narrative' to prevent us from a utopian society.

Alice had been part of these fevered debates. 'How can something that it clearly so destructive be a positive?' she would frequently ask. Something that destroyed bodies and fractured sanity? When the response wasn't abuse, or accusations of being a 'sheep', they would give her diatribes with religious fervour about the net positives of a benign overlord. Each day, it seemed more people bought into this belief, and it frustrated her. All the while, it grew. Its head was visible over the treelines, and, with that, its influence grew further.

Things took a turn for the worse. Those affected by its influence started grabbing people in the streets, forcibly taking them to the pond to receive their 'blessing'. Many died there and then, and the stench of decay rose, almost in line with the height of the creature. Others succumbed to its influence and evangelised as those that had dragged them there before.

- Praise it.

Thus began the decline of the nation, along with many others. There was no way to walk in the streets anymore if you hadn't given yourself over to the beast. The deformities meant normal people were too easy to be spotted and grabbed. Military intervention failed time and time again. How can you point a gun at something when its visage warps your senses? Drone strikes failed because of electromagnetic interference. People attempted to flee the country, only to be stopped by swathes of zealots, grabbing and taking them to the pond. Despite their disfigurements, it seemed the worshippers could still operate machinery.

They discussed the nuclear option as a last resort. The politicians that had not turned were reluctant to do this. There was no guarantee it would work, and it would likely result in killing the people they were trying to save. Hiding was the only option now. Would those that turned die over time? Would they continue to eat? Only time would tell.

Alice, still slumped against the wall, dozed. Sleep was scarce these days. Even with the makeshift barricades she'd crudely wedged against the door, she never felt safe. Her brief slumber interrupted by screaming from the street below. She peeked through the curtain. A man ran as fast as his legs allowed, pursued by five nimble zealots. She closed her eyes, and a tear fell for the man. Doomed to be caught. He would run out of breath, but they wouldn't. They would continue, only stopping if they died. Their single-minded focus only wanted one thing–for people to praise it.

Her fists screwed into balls. How long would she continue to live like this? It didn't seem like the worshippers were dying of starvation or showed any signs of slowing. She was one person, but was it possible to change the situation alone? Could she infiltrate and work from within? Or communicate with it if she approached? Why die on their terms when she should die on her own?

Alice waited until dusk. A journey on foot would result in capture in daylight hours. She'd best stick to darkness. As time passed, her mood changed. She felt excited, elated even. With all thoughts of desperation and futility pushed to the wayside, intrigue replaced it. What would she say? Would it understand? She jiggled her leg impatiently, waiting for the orange hues that would signal her departure.

As the night drew near, she grabbed her old baseball bat from the cupboard. It would be futile if several things caught her, and a mis-timed swing might not affect one of them alone, but the security made her brave. With trepidation, she pulled away furniture from her make-shift barricade, wincing at the slightest noise. Making enough room for the door to open, she scanned through the mottled glass to check for movement. There was none. She opened the door and took a step outside, a first step to what might be her end.

Alice controlled her breathing as she moved through the streets. If she glanced upwards at the thing in the distance, her body would tremor. She shielded her eyes with a hand and moved forward, avoiding glances towards her destination. The slightest noise would startle her as she clung to the shadows, listening intently for shuffling sounds or laboured breathing. The pond was three miles away. Would she even make it? Had she made a mistake?

In normal circumstances, three miles would be nothing. A brisk forty-five-minute walk, nothing more. As she crossed what she estimated to be the one-mile mark, a glance at her watch told her she'd spent an hour already.

With no encounters so far, she grew in confidence and picked up her pace, scanning the blocks ahead, then taking long, but stealthy strides towards her destination. This approach worked, and within the hour, she was close to her destination.

The stench hit Alice hard. Around the entrance to the woods, bodies were strewn. Her gag reflex was not strong enough to prevent her from emptying her stomach onto the floor with racking heaves. Figures emerged from the trees rapidly at the sound. Her right hand gripped the bat, but she raised her left hand.

-    Stop! Stop!! I'm here... I'm here to praise it.

It was a gamble, but one that seemed to pay off. As the zealots paused and allowed her to press forward, her head bowed as a gut-wrenching sense of doom gripped her. She pulled her t-shirt over her nose to disguise the foul aroma of decay with that of her own body odour. She stepped lightly over the dead, partially out of respect, but also to keep the rot from her clothing in the slim chance she walked away from this. Despite her fatalism, a glimmer of hope remained that the nightmare could be over.

Her head pulsed with every step forward. She could see the base of the creature, so she closed her eyes, pushing her hands out to avoid trees and pressed on, blind. The pulse grew in intensity. After a few moments, she pivoted, facing the opposite direction, and used her peripheral vision to judge where she was. She noted the edge of the pond, a few more steps, and she'd have been flailing in the water. She inhaled. Now was the time.

- Can you see me?

Alice spoke into the night air. There was no response, no change to the pulsing in her head. She repeated her question at an increased volume. Still nothing. She screwed her eyes tight and span back, facing the pond. She heard the gentle splashes as the beast shifted its weight.

- What do you want?

Her query again yielded no response. If she opened her eyes, would she become like those things? She had to try. Slowly, she took in what lay before her. It was magnificent. Up close, she could see each individual scale shimmering with moisture evaporating from the pond. Colours danced in front of her eyes as she gazed upwards. It was at least four storeys high and like nothing she'd ever seen before. Beautiful in its monstrosity. Four chunky limbs planted it firmly in the waters, the torso tapered outwards up to another four arms hanging by its side. Each 'hand' had two fingers and the semblance of a thumb. The head was mouthless, widening at its peak into a carapace that shielded the glowing green eyes, all of which pointed in the opposite direction of Alice. She trembled uncontrollably, and with a lot of effort, she repeated her question again?

- WHAT DO YOU WANT FROM US?

The creature did not respond or look in her direction. She could hear voices from the trees; she was not alone.

-    Praise it. Praise it. Praise it.

Alice's nose bled, her t-shirt clinging to her body as it became drenched in her blood. She couldn't move her arms or legs to move away. Her right eyebrow drooped, stretching down to her cheek, her body vibrating on the spot as her nerve endings screamed pain across her face. She had little time left.

-    Look... at... meeeee!!!

With her remaining eye, she looked upwards, pleading with the beast to acknowledge her presence. If she was to die, she at least wanted to know why. It didn't turn, it didn't even notice she was there. It sat staring into the distance, blank to her cries. Alice gurgled as blood erupted from her mouth, mixing with the stream from her nose. Her hair floated down her body as it fell out in clumps. Her scalp bubbled, cascading flesh over her remaining eye. She dropped to the ground, painful last breaths escaping through her gaping mouth. The zealots in the trees walked away.

Acknowledgements.

As ever, a big thank you to Matthew at the Globe Café for allowing us to host our nights every Tuesday. If you are reading this, and are in the area, feel free to pop along.

Also, a big thanks to everyone that contributed to this anthology. We have had so many submissions, making it the beefiest one yet! Each author has been responsible for writing and editing their own work and they have done a great job.

And thanks to you, the reader. Buying this book supports and encourages fledgling authors and gives a boost to those that are already published too! Each author's name is below their story, so if you are interested in further works, look on Amazon to find what they have published and enjoy those books too! At the time of publishing (October 2021), Ants Ambridge, Gemma Owen-Kendall, Mark Sandford, Grace King, Rebekah Richards and Lord Stabdagger all have works available, but no doubt more will be added in the future!

Happy Halloween!

Printed in Great Britain
by Amazon